A
Harlequin
Romance

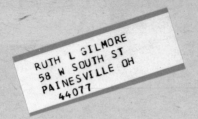

DEDICATION JONES

DEDICATION JONES

by

KATE NORWAY

H A R L E Q U I N   B O O K S
Winnipeg • Canada   New York • New York

DEDICATION JONES

First published in 1969 by Mills & Boon Limited,
17 - 19 Foley Street, London, England.

Harlequin Canadian edition published December, 1970
Harlequin U.S. edition published March, 1971

Standard Book Number: 373-51449-2.

Printed in Canada

CHAPTER ONE

LEANING against the wall outside Matron's office I knew exactly what was going on inside. Caradoc Hughes was standing there, in his spanking new smock—as stiff and bulging with shrinkage-allowance as my new dress—with *Staff Nurse* embroidered in blue on the pen-pocket, looking out over Matron's sunk head to the new-look flats.

Originally, I suppose, the King Edward VII Memorial Hospital was meant to serve the dark tide of slum terraces flooding to its boundary walls, and to dominate them architecturally. But by the time I'd joined nearly all the grimy little houses had gone. Some had been bombed or burned flat years before and their graves purpled over with willowherb. Most had been bulldozed down by the lumbering yellow earth-movers of contractors like Bright, Richards, and Lockyer before they erected brittle towers of luxury flats, laid smooth green carpets about them, and decorated the night sky with their slotted columns of light.

Before the war—so Home Sister used to tell us—Matron's office had stared across a glass-spiked wall at the rusty outbuildings of a chrome-plating factory, and the desk had come to face the door rather than the view. It still did, in spite of Miss Hurcombe's retirement and the fresh green and white vista, because Miss Carte was a tactician. We reckoned she preferred any harsh daylight that was going to fall on the young faces of her visitors rather than on her own ageing skin. Besides, too much light provoked her photophobia so that she had to take off her glasses and dab her eyes, which was scarcely an authoritative gesture however briskly performed.

She would, I knew, be crouching there with her head half-lifted from her interminable lists, frowning up at Caradoc. I could hear the rumble of her voice, no more, but Alice

Ratleigh—who was next to the door—could hear what was being said. It evidently didn't please her. 'He *would* ask for Surgical,' she grumbled softly. She looked as discontented as only dark narrow girls can. 'He knows perfectly well——'

And then Caradoc marched out miming brow-mopping, and strawberry pink below his red hair, and Ratleigh bustled in and closed the door. Caradoc said: 'Hi, Didi. Wind's east—watch it!' and went on down the corridor. I moved nearer to the door. The wind usually was in the east where Miss Carte was concerned. I had never known it back round except when Rose Innes's father had died in the private wing. Even then it had been barely a week before she was blowing Rose out backwards for wearing sheer black nylons instead of the regulation thirty-denier. Maybe she couldn't help it: she was reputed to suffer from hypertension. I dare say I'd have poured out adrenalin myself if I'd had all her responsibility.

I could hear her voice rising. 'I know, Staff Nurse. I know. But I've no surgical vacancy. I *know* you asked for surgical work. Most of you newly registered people have asked to go to the surgical side. It's always the way! I've nothing left now but Women's Medical, Geriatric, Isolation, or night relief.'

I could imagine Ratleigh's reaction. She would be wanting to tell Matron exactly what to do with her old ladies. And she wouldn't want night relief either. Ratleigh liked to have the glow of power about her, helping to run a ward, coping with relatives and training schedules, and all the other sisterly jobs. Night relief, not knowing where you'd be from one night to the next, sometimes filling in for a junior night sister, sometimes taking theatre or charge of a ward, or stuck down in Casualty half the night with no meal-relief, wasn't her cup of tea at all. She would surely ask for Isolation. I was surprised when she said resignedly: 'Oh, night relief, then, Matron.'

'Very well.' Miss Carte's voice had a sharp edge. 'Of course, you're not *compelled* to stay on and do any staffing at all, if you'd prefer to go elsewhere. But after we've trained you for three years . . .' I let that wash over me. Peptalk number three, I told myself. We all know we owe Teddy's a lot. It's when people keep labouring the point that the idea gets tedious.

'But if a surgical vacancy *should* crop up I'd still like to be considered,' Ratleigh persisted. I wished she would just bow out gracefully and forget it. I was in a hurry. If I knew anything about the students in Ward Five not one of them would have thought of doing the four-hourlies or the swabbings, and it was already time for Miss Fantague's round. Her house surgeon, Andy Gilpin, was hovering in the front hall waiting for her to come striding out of the consultants' cloakroom; and with Sister Chinnery on holiday, and Staff Perrott in charge for the second week running, it was likely to be a prickly round in any case. Miss Fantague was a superb gynaecologist, but she was a demon for protocol and she considered it beneath her dignity to be attended by a mere staff nurse and made no bones about showing it.

Staff Perrott had begged me to hurry, or to leave it until another day. 'But I can't!' I'd told her. 'She-who-must-be-obeyed has spoken. My name's on the office list, and fail not at my peril. If I don't go she'll think I don't mean to stay on.'

Then I heard my own name. 'No, Matron. There's only Nurse—Staff Nurse Jones,' Ratleigh was saying. There were dozens of Joneses, and I wasn't surprised when Matron asked which one. 'D. D. Jones, Matron. She's the last.' I wasn't, in fact, because a scared-looking junior had edged up beside me trying not to crease a breakages requisition form. Ratleigh's voice was close to the door now. She rolled up her eyes when she came out. 'Medical, Geriatric,' she muttered disgustedly. 'And I asked her *weeks* ago for Surgical! Charming.' She flounced off down the corridor to the wards, holding her cap on with one hand, and the green light came on again on Matron's door panel.

While I waited for Miss Carte to lay down her scratching pen I put my hands behind my back and gazed out at the giraffe-necked crane winging an earth-bucket between and beyond two of the white towers. It had a red and white enamelled label on it, halfway up the jib, and though I couldn't read it at that distance I knew it said *B.R.L.* Bright, Richards, and Lockyer. Geoff's firm—or rather, his father's. Bright and Richards had been dead for years and Geoff would be joining the board when we married. If he had his way that would be quite soon. Only I wasn't at all sure that I wanted it to be soon. It was going to be a wrench, leaving

9

Teddy's, and Geoff didn't approve of wives who worked. He didn't understand, I told myself. Teddy's wasn't like a shop, or an office. It was a life.

'Well, Staff Nurse?'

Matron was looking up at me, waiting. 'I'm sorry, Matron,' I said quickly. 'I was miles away.'

'That was obvious.' She didn't smile. I'd known she wouldn't. It had been an idiotic thing to say. 'I hope you're not "miles away" when you're about your work? ... I suppose *you* want to go to a surgical ward too? Do you?'

'No, Matron.' What was it the others in my set had said? Jean Moss, I knew, wanted to get more medical experience. And Rose Innes wanted to go to nights, because there would be a junior night sister's vacancy coming up pretty soon. That left Isolation and Geriatric. 'I'll go wherever I'm needed, Matron. But I'd rather not go to Women's Medical because——'

'Because you've no patience with women, I suppose? Like the rest of your set!'

It wasn't like that at all. 'No, Matron, but——'

'But you're more interested in surgery? Or a *male* ward?'

I could feel my face getting hot, and I knew very well it was rhododendron pink. Why did she always have to get in some crack about *men*? 'No, it's just that someone else is hoping for that, and I think she's more suitable than I am, Matron.'

She clearly didn't believe that for a minute, but she said: 'Very well, then I shall send you to Isolation. There'll be two of you. Mr. Hughes and yourself.'

Why couldn't she just say 'Staff Nurse Hughes'? She made it plain enough that she didn't like male nurses, I reflected. And at the prize-giving it had been 'these girls' in her speech, and 'finest profession for women'. No wonder Ken Demmery had turned crimson when he'd gone up to the platform for his paediatrics prize, and it proved to be a thick volume on baby management. Maybe the girls were right, and Matron had rigged that deliberately. 'I see,' I said. 'Thank you, Matron.'

'You do *want* to stay on?' Her cod-cold eyes dared me to deny it. 'I understand you're engaged to be married.'

I said I was. 'But I don't want to leave yet, Matron.' That was true, but I couldn't keep Geoff waiting a lot longer. If only he would have agreed to my carrying on for a while after we were married ... 'And I may be able to do part-time after I'm married.' No, he would never agree to it. Never. He would think it *infra dig* for his wife to work. I should have to make the break before long. Only not yet.

'And so I should hope, Staff Nurse! It's quite disgraceful the way you girls waste your training, rushing off to get married the moment you have your registration. This is what all your training had been leading up to—taking responsibility, and helping to train the students!'

'Yes, Matron.' I knew. But explaining that to Geoff was a different matter. 'I want to stay as long as I can, of course.'

'Very well, you can report to Isolation after lunch. And, Staff Nurse ...'

'Yes, Matron?'

'Remember that you'll now have authority. Remember you *are* a State Registered Nurse, and that the student nurses will look to you for discipline. See that you exercise it.'

Authority? Discipline? If she meant throwing my weight about she could forget it. The patients were what mattered, in my eyes, not keeping the students in line. That was the ward sister's job. Anyhow, there weren't any students in Isolation. Not junior ones, anyhow. I was blowed if I was going to discipline third-years like Serpell and Robson, only two sets junior to me. There hadn't been any first- or second-years down there since they'd stopped using the place for infectious cases, and turned it into what sounded like a ragbag of odd cases that couldn't be classified. 'Yes, Matron,' I said obediently.

Up in Ward Five Staff Perrott was dithering at the first bed facing Miss Fantague's pouter pigeon bosom, and Andy Gilpin was leaning on the bottom rail, drooping to bring himself down to their level. At the far end of the ward Nurse Packer, our second-year, was trundling a screen back into its corner. To judge from her slithering cap, the mask still dangling round her neck, and the jumbled trolley askew by Mrs. Cooksey's bed, she had just scrambled her way through the last of the swabbings. That let me out. I glanced at Staff Perrott and she gave me a nervous little neck jerk that meant: 'Stand by, tidy the beds after us, and look intelligent for God's sake. The Fantail's on the war-path.'

I nodded, and hung around behind Andy. Too close, as it happened, because when he straightened up his elbow hit me in the eye. He said: 'Sorry, Nurse. Didn't see you.' Perrott looked jittery. Miss Fantague pushed past me and snapped, 'Good heavens, girl, don't get in the *way*. You asked for that.' That was a big help. After I had straightened Miss Baxter's bed I kept my distance, except when Perrott signalled wildly for a clean speculum or a request form, or the P.V. tray.

It wasn't until the round was over and the Fantail was heading, bust first, for the doctors' handbasin, that I noticed there were no clean towels on the shelf. I cursed Packer and her mate Barsby, tore along to the linen room for a fresh supply of what the inventory called huckaback-doctors-for-the-use-of, and managed to canter back in time to push one at the Fantail just as she dripped off her hands and looked up at the empty shelf. She frowned. 'Any need for all this galloping about, Nurse Jones?' She stood there drying her hands, fiddling about with the cuticles and looking at me as though I'd just asked her for a termination on social grounds. 'You're not on the hockey field now.' Then her eyebrows went up as she noticed my new dress. 'Oh? We're a *staff* nurse now, are we? Well, it's time we cultivated a little decorum, isn't it? Or we shall be unpopular in this ward.'

'I'm sorry,' I said, 'but I'm not staying here, Miss Fantague. I'm going to Isolation.' That was actually audience information for Staff Perrott, because I knew she was dying to hear what Matron had cooked up for me.

The Fantail laughed in a funny way and looked across at Andy. 'I see. Off to the faith-healing department, hm?'

Andy winked at me with the eye away from her and said he didn't think it was a bad scheme. 'After all,' he added, 'look at the psychosomatic backaches we get up here. Oh, they turn out to be retroverted sometimes, yes. But there must be thousands of R.U.s going about who *don't* have backache. More often than not it's plain marital frustration.'

That was an unfortunate remark, to say the least, because Miss Baxter, in the nearest bed, wasn't suffering from marital frustration or any other kind. She had five children by an assortment of fathers, and she was no more retroverted then than the Fantail's bosom, but her low back pains were bad enough for us to have to shoot pethidine into her most evenings. She heard what Andy said, all right, and responded by flinging her *Woman's Realm* on to the floor and bouncing right under her blankets.

'Rot!' Miss Fantague said crisply. '*My* patients aren't lead-swingers.'

I don't know whether the new blue dress gave me courage, or whether it was just that I was leaving Ward Five for good and didn't much care any more, but I cut in with: 'It's not a question of lead-swinging, surely? Not consciously. Psychosomatic pain's real enough. Nobody runs up a temp. of a hundred and four by willpower.'

The Fantail threw down her towel irritably. 'The voice of the expert!' she said. 'Dear me, you *are* going to the right ward, Staff Nurse Jones.' She put my name in heavy quotes. 'Now we shall see where all the over-prescribing goes on, shan't we? *You're* not going to improve the turnover rate, are you?' She stamped off to the door, and Andy reached out to open it for her because Perrott was too shocked to move.

When they had gone Perrott skittered into the kitchen after me. 'Jones, you *are* awful!' she burst out. 'I don't know how you dare argue with that woman. She terrifies me. I go all hemiplegic at the sight of her.'

'I don't know why,' I said. I filled the kettle and put it on to boil. 'She's only a woman, after all. Same like you and me, only older. She isn't infallible, the old dragon. I quite agree with Andy—a lot of her cases *are* psychomatic. Either they've gone off their husbands, or they're scared rigid of having any more children, or Mummy never told them about the birds and bees. Anyway, they do have all sorts of aches and pains as an excuse to get out of their "wifely duties", let's face it. Look at that poor little Mrs. Hurrell, for a start. Six stone four, with a little girl's voice and built like a deer—and have you *seen* that great booming gorilla she's married to? Hands like legs of lamb! *I'd* have undiagnosable backache too, if I were married to that.'

Andy stood at the door laughing. He leaned on the

doorpost and shook. 'Have you seen the Fantail's wee man?'

We all knew that Miss Fantague's real name was now Mrs. Mossop, off duty, but none of us knew anything about her spouse. 'We'll buy it,' I said. 'Tell us, Andy.'

He held one hand horizontally across the middle button of his white coat, and then drew both forefingers downwards at about three inches apart. 'And she's terrified of him,' he said.

Perrott didn't believe a word of it. 'Oh, really, Mr. Gilpin! How you do exaggerate!'

'Not a word of a lie,' he assured her. 'He's around five foot three, weighs about as much as little Jones here, and it's yes-darling, no-darling, three-bags-full-darling from her when he's about.'

'Good for him,' I said. 'I'm glad *somebody* doesn't let her ride roughshod.'

'He's a bank inspector,' Andy went on, 'whatever that may be. I gather the very term strikes fear into the hearts of husky golfing branch managers. He plays off about four, so he must have something, damn it . . . Do I smell tea?'

Perrott lifted her own nose. 'Pour your own, Mr. Gilpin. We've other things to do, beside running after housemen.'

'You surprise me.' He reached for a cup and filled it. 'Such as what, for instance?'

'Such as organising this ward so that it'll run without *me*, for a start,' I told him. 'Do you realise——'

'Ah, of course. You're going to be one of Dr. Jones's young ladies, aren't you?'

'I've no idea,' I said. 'I can't make out what *does* go on down in Iso these days. They seem to have all sorts of things down there—skins, medical, surgical, the lot. I should think Sister Ross must wish she had a straightforward ward . . . What did the Fantail mean—faith-healing?'

'It's all happening down there,' Andy declared. 'Iso's the swinging place these days. As for Theo Ross, she's in her element. Worshipping at the shrine, so to speak.'

Sister Ross was leaning against a plasterer's trestle, looking at the five new cubicles at the end of the isolation block. 'They'll be ready for us in a week,' she told me. 'The furniture requisition's gone in; the bedding's arrived; the curtains are in my office. It's going to be interesting, taking Dr. Jones's people.' She had that look in her eyes.

'Dr. Jones?' I said. 'You don't mean—you mean Dr. Ffestin-Jones? The psychiatrist?'

'I do.' She was still young enough to spread her lashes at me in a way that said *he* interested her, rather than his patients. 'The Secretary's just been down to talk about it. All the diagnosed infections are being sent on now, as you know. So we're just holding a couple of cubicles for queries. Then we need two or three for people who need to be isolated *from* infection—leukaemias and whatnot. Well, it's far easier to barrier-nurse them down here than in the main block side-wards. We're keeping as many as necessary from time to time for sick staff: that's to release more side-wards for amenity cases. And all the rest—except for these beds of Dr. Jones's—are for referred cases from the wards, sent for his opinion. Cases the other consultants think may be psychomatic. Functional things, and untraceable pains and so forth. See?'

I hadn't realised that there was a plan. It had seemed to me that Isolation was being filled up with all kinds of overflow oddments lately, without rhyme or reason. 'Then it'll be largely a psychotherapy unit? Aren't we doing the Nerve Hospital out of a job?'

'Not really, no. They're not just *straight* psycho cases. They've all got some other condition ... Well, young Hughes is keen if you aren't, Staff !' I think she mistook my baffled expression for lack of interest.

'But I *am*,' I said quickly. 'Heavens, I've been saying for long enough that they don't pay enough attention to that aspect here. And that if G.P.s would take a bit more time out to——'

'All right.' She stood upright again and led the way back to her office, her arms folded in a purposeful way. 'One thing, Staff, I'm glad I got you and not that Ratleigh girl. She thinks of nothing but surgery. Plain carpentry and no nonsense, that's her line. No imagination whatsoever.'

'She's gone to night relief,' I said.

'And where's your mate Innes?'

'She wants nights too, so I expect she'll get it. They can never get enough S.R.N.s who really like it ... She's after

Sister Humpherson's job, when she gets married.'

'Well, I hope *you* don't want to go haring off? How anyone can swop this job for a dull suburban life I can't think.' She turned to face me. 'Oh, I forgot. You're engaged.' She said it heavily.

'Yes,' I agreed, 'but not in a hurry. *I* don't want a "dull suburban life", anyway. And I shall cry when I leave.'

'Will you? Yes, perhaps you will. Look at me, nearly forty and still here. I did mean to marry, and then when it came to the push I couldn't bear to go. Everyone thought I was stupid not to grab him. After all, he's a consultant now. I could be having the good life, I suppose. Still, it's done now. I don't really regret it.' She'd said that, or something like it, to a lot of people in her time. Nobody seemed to know whether it was an act or the truth, but I thought it was probably true. She was an attractive woman, and she was also a good nurse, and I could imagine that the choice had been agony.

The phone was ringing. By the time we got to the office Caradoc had answered it. He ran into us outside the door and recoiled apologising. 'Sorry, it's an admission, Sister. A Hodgkins', been in before. Tony Sugden. Do you remember him? They said in Cas that you would.'

'Oh, Tony! Yes, of course ... I don't know how that laddie keeps going, but he does. It must be ... yes, it's his fifth year. Poor boy!'

'Fifth?' Caradoc wrinkled his forehead incredulously. 'He can't have long to go, then. I mean, by the fourth year, ninety per cent——'

'Oh, rubbish!' Sister Ross was almost pretty when she was flushed. 'In the present state of our knowledge, maybe not. But they're researching like mad on this, Hughes. It can't be long before there's a breakthrough ... Put him in Room Three, will you?'

'Yes, Sister. Only why's he in Iso?'

'To keep bugs away from him,' I put in. 'Lord, he can't risk an infection, not even a coryza. That'd put paid to him. Best place for him.'

'Oh. Well, I've never nursed one before.'

'You'll learn,' Sister told him. 'And put some flowers in his room. Take those silly carnations out of my office. He likes flowers, and they're in my way. You go in and read

16

the report, Jones. I'm off at four. I've got a date in the dental clinic. . . . Impacted wisdom, at my age!'

I wished she wouldn't go on about her age, and being on the shelf, and all the rest of it. She was better looking than any of the youngsters, and she still had a flash in her eye when she liked. Especially when the men were around. I wondered who the consultant was, the man she might have married. Everyone said it must be Mr. Davidson, because she used to run Ward Three before she had Isolation, but I couldn't believe that. He wasn't her sort; he was too dry a stick for her. Besides, he had married an Italian girl, met while he was in the R.A.M.C., and Sister Ross couldn't have been a day over sixteen at the time.

'Tell me about Tony Sugden,' I said.

She shrugged. 'Not much to tell. He's a Hodgkins'. His blood picture's pretty funny. It began when he was fourteen—and now he's nineteen. Ninety-odd to one that he could still be with us, but he is. He's a nice laddie, too. He gets an exacerbation every few weeks, febrile attacks, fresh glands up, bubbly lungs, and so on; comes in, gets shots of this and that—nitrogen mustard usually—and goes out again . . . Only one of these times he won't go home. It's always touch and go. In between times he's fine. Helps his people on a farm, drives the tractor, and the Land-Rover, and you'd never know. Except that he's beginning to get a bit moonfaced with steroids, you wouldn't think he'd ever had a day's illness.'

'What filthy luck,' I said. 'Does he have an idea?'

'I don't know. I dare say he has. He isn't stupid, and he knows what drugs he has, and he's quite capable of looking them up in the library. He's interested, you see. He could do a cut-down better than most of the housemen by now. His family know the score, of course.' She straightened her shoulders again. 'Well, this won't get the baby a new dress! Time we thought about teas. Jones, you do the sick nurses, will you? Serpell and Robson can do the others. All light diet except Stanway, and she can have anything she fancies.'

'Stanway?' I looked up. 'You mean Stanway with red hair? What is she?' I was still finding my way down the reports and I hadn't reached her.

'U.O., at the moment. Lump on the back of her head. It doesn't hurt, doesn't fluctuate, no history of a bump. X-rays don't show much. She came down here as query glandular fever, but I'll swear that's miles off the beam.'

'Have they done a biopsy, Sister?'

'Yes, but we haven't had the report yet. Why?'

'That's quite a question,' I said. 'Let's hope we're wrong. She's a nice kid.'

I remembered Stanway. I'd worked with her. She'd always been the picture of health, even if she did carry puppyfat. I went on hoping I was wrong about her. That, and the Sugden boy too, didn't seem fair.

Two of the sick nurses, Rutherford and Hillman, were post-op appendicectomies. They were sitting up, and they were fine. The third, a pretty little P.T.S. intake named Bache, whom I didn't remember having seen before, was sobbing under her blankets. I checked her notes before I said anything. Renal colic, query renal calculus, query ureteric stricture. Only no evidence. Intravenous pyelogram —clear. Cholecystogram—clear. Retrograde—clear. Blood count, normal, like everything else. I said: 'Come on, old dear. What's wrong? Pain? Let's look.'

She nodded and rammed one fist into her back, thumb first. It certainly looked like renal colic. Her pulse was racing too. 'All right,' I told her. 'I'll get you something for that. Try to relax.' That was a counsel of perfection, I knew. Renal colic is just about the worst pain there is. I'd seen tough policemen crying with it. 'Shan't be two ticks.' There wasn't anything written up for her, and I went along to Sister Ross in the office.

'What now?' she wanted to know. 'Time I went.'

I explained. 'Doesn't seem to be anything written up,' I added. 'What can I give her?'

'Oh, just one codeine.' She finished tidying her stationary rack, and then looked up. Well? What are you waiting for?

'Codeine?' I said. 'One codeine, Sister?'

'That's what I said.'

'You can't mean it! For renal colic?' I was sure she'd made a mistake. 'I'd have thought she needed pethidine, or morph.'

'Would you? Yes, well, just give her a codeine. Oh, and tell her it's one of the special tablets we got from Manchester.'

I was beginning to think that one of us was off her head,

18

but I took one five-grain codeine tablet and a glass of water, and made Bache swallow it. 'Is it one of the special ones?' she wanted to know.

'From Manchester,' I nodded. 'That's right. That ought to help.' If it did, I was a Dutchman, I thought.

Approximately ten seconds after she had downed it—it must just about have reached her stomach—she sat up and smiled. It was like one of those television faces changing when the pile-driving hammer of headache is replaced, in a wavy dissolve, by a caressing hand. 'Oh, gosh, that's *marvellous*, Staff! I thought I was going to die. That *ghastly* pain!'

'I know,' I said. 'Gone now?'

She nodded, and her silvery fluff of hair fell over her hot little face. 'Yes, thanks. Those tablets are terrific. What are they called? Do you know?'

'No idea,' I lied. 'Ask Sister. Like some tea now?'

'I'd love some.'

'Anything to eat?'

'Golly, yes! I'm simply *starving*. Could I have egg and tomato sandwiches?'

'I'll see what we can do,' I promised. Then I went back to tackle Sister. I felt like slapping her hard.

She was laughing when I walked in. 'Well? Instant recovery?'

'Quicker than that,' I said.

'And I'll bet she eats a whacking great tea.'

'She's asking for egg and tomato sandwiches, yes.'

'There you are, then. *Now* do we need a psychosomatic unit down here?'

'But she was in agony! Her pulse was all over the place, and she was——'

'I know. She's been here a week. Oh, she *has* the pain all right. It's real enough to her.'

I leaned on the edge of the desk. 'Why "the special tablets from Manchester"?'

'Now there I can't help you. What goes on between her and Dr. Jones isn't my business. That was his order and that's what I do. Ours not to reason why. He may give dotty instructions, but he seems to know what he's doing.'

'Yes. Well, she's asking what the tablets are called. I told her to ask you.'

'Ah. Then I shan't go in, so she can't. And by the time I've gone I dare say Dr. Jones will be here, so let him handle it. Tell him she's asking. I dare say it'll mean something significant to him if it doesn't to us!'

'I'll do that,' I said. 'Meantime, she gets the sandwiches, does she?'

'Oh yes. She's down as "light diet", but give her what she fancies ... How's Stanway?'

'I've not been in yet. I'll do her last.'

'Well, if her head aches she'd better have something. Now I'm off. Can you and Hughes cope?'

'We'll cope,' I said. I wasn't at all sure that we could, but at least there were two of us. 'Any message for Dr. Jones, Sister?'

'Yes. Tell him he's wonderful, and if he can keep the Bache child from pestering the night nurses so much the better.'

I smiled at her. 'I'll just mention Nurse Bache,' I said. 'We don't want him to get a swelled head, do we? There's nothing more unbearable than a consultant too big for his boots.' Then I thought of the Fantail, and added: 'Or hers.'

She slung her cape over one shoulder and went to the door. 'Ah, Miss Fantague. Well, I can promise you Dr. Jones is nothing like *her*, Staff.'

I hoped she was right.

CHAPTER TWO

I GOT in to look at Stanway ten minutes later, after I'd settled little Bache. She was lying flat, looking at the ceiling, but she sat up when she saw me. The first thing that struck me was that she'd lost an awful lot of weight. She had been plump, to say the least, when I'd worked with her in Skins six months before, and now her clavicles were prominent and her wrists were like sticks. She said: 'Hi. Nice to see *you* again. Are you here for good?'

'For a time, anyway,' I said. 'How goes it?'

She rubbed the back of her head and frowned. 'It doesn't, that's the trouble. The blasted thing's getting bigger, if you ask me. Well, feel it for yourself.'

I did. It was hard, and it didn't move, and it was as big as a duck egg, only knobbly. 'How come?' I said. 'Someone have a go at you with a rolling pin?'

'Not a thing. I've never even bumped my head under a bed-frame picking up kirbigrips for the ruddy women in Ward One. It just arrived, uninvited. Actually I thought it was maybe a rheumatic nodule at first, but it can't be.'

'Maybe it is, though,' I suggested. 'I've seen plenty of them worse than that.' That was a lie, too. That made several in one afternoon, and I didn't even have my fingers crossed. But after three years I no longer had quite the same pangs of conscience when I invented such tarradiddles. Nurses can't afford that sort of conscience. I dare say we shall all be forgiven at the final reckoning, and if we're not it will have been worth it. 'Yes, that's what it *must* be, Stanway. You're a rheumaticky old lady.'

Stanway looked at me pityingly. 'Come off it, Jones. Just because you're a staff nurse ... I've *worked* with Dr. Watterson's rheumatics, and I'm not stupid.'

I might have known I'd be wasting my time. 'Well, what

is it, then?' A silly question, but she was going to tell me in any case.

'You know what *I* think?'

'What?' I went to look out at the open casement. The lawn outside needed cutting, and there was an old forgotten grey tennis ball lying in the middle of the path. It looked as desolate as I felt, waiting for Stanway to say it.

'My guess is that it's a sarcoma.' She was quite matter-of-fact about it, and that shook me far more than if she'd been emotional.

'Oh, tripe!' I said. I swung round. 'Look, what do you want for tea?'

'What is there?'

'Salady things, cream sponge, blackberry jam.'

'No protein?'

'You can have a boiled egg, I suppose. Or egg salad. But there'll be supper at seven, don't forget.'

'Boiled egg then, please. I've got a thing about this, you see. All the proteins you can absorb, that's the way to fight back at the beast. In the end the pirate cells get fed up and chuck it. Jones, it's been *proved*. There's a woman in America——'

'You're cracked,' I said unsteadily. 'Give me five minutes to lay it on.'

I took her two boiled eggs, in fact, and a cheese sandwich too. If that was the way she felt there was nothing to do but play along with her.

I met Caradoc as I was coming out again, and he said: 'Now Sister's hopped it, I suppose you're in charge? You're a set senior to me.' He gave me a mock salute with a lot of hand-quivering. 'Yes, ma'am!'

'Ass,' I said. 'Why don't we have a cuppa too? Have you done all your chores?'

'Just about. Robson's finishing the rank and file, and I've sent Serpell to tea, and I've admitted Tony whatsit. He's had a cup of tea, but he doesn't feel like food. O.K.?'

'I'll look in,' I promised. 'But listen, you'll have to watch what you say to Stanway, if you bump into her. She's quite frank about it—she's made up her mind she's got a sarcoma, and she's got a theory that bags of protein'll shoot it down. She made my blood run cold, the way she talked. So don't register shock if she says anything to you . . . Yes, let's have some tea.'

We sat on the kitchen table drinking our tea, and Nurse Robson came to join us. She'd been in Isolation for half a change already, she said, and what did we think of it?

Caradoc said it was great, and that Sister Ross wasn't at all a bad sort; and I said: 'What hits me right between the eyes is the difference between Stanway's attitude and little Bache's.'

Robson was like a bushbaby anyway, but she widened her eyes more than ever. 'You're telling me, Staff. Shakes you, doesn't it? There's young Bache screaming in agony, thinking she's clogged up with kidney stones, and behaving as if she is too—and there's poor old Stanway being as down-to-earth as you like. And I'll bet that *is* a sarcoma. It just isn't fair, is it? She's a nice girl. *And* a darn good nurse.'

'Bache hasn't had time to blot her copybook yet, either,' I pointed out. 'So why the kickup? If it was plain ornery home-sickness she'd go home, not come in here and cry her eyes out.'

Robson shrugged. 'Maybe she just doesn't like nursing. Sorry she joined or something, and doesn't like to say so. And she could be homesick and too proud to admit it. You can't tell what goes on in the minds of the Lambs. Half of them are potty.'

'I can,' I said. 'I'm not so old that I don't remember being a Lamb myself, if you are. With me it was having to share a room—we had to when I joined, because they hadn't finished the New Home. And the girl I was with—she left at the end of P.T.S.—used to cry all night and eat toffees. The floor would be knee-deep in toffee papers in the mornings. Sort of comfort-eating. Anyhow, I hated sharing—I'm practically an only child; Freda's five years older than I am, and I'd never had to—and I used to cry too, and I used to plan to run away, only I never had any money so it didn't come to anything.'

'What did you do with your money?' Caradoc wanted to know.

'Oh, I used to lend it to my room-mate to buy toffees and things, and I hardly ever got it back. I must have been a bit dim in those days.'

Caradoc grinned. 'Talking of room-mates ... Ken Demmery's room's next to mine, and the night before the finals I could hear all this talking going on in there, and I thought it was a bit much. I banged the wall, and it still went on, and in the end I went marching in and said: "Haven't you any rooms of your own to go to?" And there was Ken, fast asleep, reciting the spinal nerves. You know, "On Old Olympus' Towering Top . . ." All that rigmarole.'

'A Finn And German Viewed Some Hops,' I finished. 'Oculomotor, Olfactory, Optic—I can *never* remember which comes first.'

Robson was interested. 'Oh, *we* didn't learn that. Ours was "Outrageous Olive Ought To Tickle Albert's Feet And Give Victoria Sick Headaches." Still, you had old Miss Lucas, didn't you? We had the Juggernaut. She had the dottiest mnemonics for everything. Like—mitral valve, mitre, bishop, cardinal, red, left. So the mitral valve's on the left. Crazy.'

'And *we* learned: "On Olga's Old Trapeze There Are Five Acrobats Gutting Very Small Herrings," ' said a quietly amused voice at the kitchen door.

I stood up quickly and dabbed my cup into the sink. The other two scattered and left me alone with him. I had only seen those dark intent eyes once before at close quarters, and that had been in my first year, but I had not forgotten them. The recognition was a warm little shock, like a bass guitar string plucked unexpectedly in the dark. 'I'm so sorry, Dr. Ffestin-Jones,' I said. 'I didn't hear you come in.' I smoothed my apron and felt to see whether my cap was straight.

'Plain Dr. Jones will be enough for everyday use.' He smiled down at me. He was tallish, but not nearly as tall as Geoff, and he had strong, compact-looking shoulders and well-brushed sepia hair with a suppressed kink. His voice still kept its native clarity and pure vowel sounds, for all its softness. It did the thing to me that North Walian voices always do, the thing that the smell of peat-smoky Harris tweed does too, and the feel of cat-fur and the colour of delphiniums. It is something that begins in my toes and throat, and explodes at some internal meeting point. He went on: 'I didn't mean to eavesdrop . . . Are you in charge just now?'

'Yes, sir. Sister's off.' I thumbed my identity badge forward for him to read. 'I'm staffing here now.'

He bent to look at the typed slip behind its cellophane window and smiled again. 'I see. That makes two of us. I shall remember that easily enough ... Well, Staff Nurse D. D. Jones—shall we call on Nurse Bache now? How has she been?'

'She came up with a fairly bad lumbar pain about half an hour ago,' I said. 'One codeine had quite a dramatic effect.'

'Ah, yes. The "special tablet", I suppose?' We began to walk along the corridor side by side. 'Next time it won't even be codeine. It'll be a chalk tablet.'

'A placebo? Why Manchester, sir?' I wanted to know.

'Why *not* Manchester? I could have said Liverpool, or Birmingham, or Bourton-on-the-Water. It added authenticity, you see.'

I didn't see at all, but I said: 'Yes, sir. So you think this is a purely hysterical pain? Is that it?'

He moved his head doubtfully. 'I don't really like the word "hysteria". I very rarely use it. I think maybe she has a ureteric spasm that's psychogenic in origin. Not quite the same thing.' He paused outside Bache's door. 'There's no need to come in and chaperone me, thank you, Staff.'

It seemed to me that if Bache was the imaginative kind he was taking something of a risk, but it wasn't my job to say so. I left him to it.

I looked in at the Hodgkins' boy after that. Caradoc and Serpell were fixing his bed, and he looked pretty feverish. Caradoc said: 'We'd better get some one to see him, hadn't we? I know he was seen in Cas on admission, but his temp's gone up since then. Who do I get? Somebody'll have to write him up for stuff, and he's supposed to be under Dr. Watterson.'

'Right. I'll see if I can get his registrar,' I promised.

I had Dr. Hastri bleeped right away. When he came on the line he said: 'Look, I'm tied right up in One. Can't you get the H.P.?' But Miss Sadler said she was tied up in Two, and surely I could get the registrar. By the time I'd tracked down the S.M.O. and he'd said he'd be over in half an hour, Dr. Hastri arrived himself, so I had to cancel the S.M.O. and Miss Sadler and leave Caradoc to deal with him.

When I finally managed to get away, at a quarter past five, he was still there, but I had left Caradoc, and Tina

Robson, and Mrs. Doherty—who was mountainous enough to make three normal orderlies—to cope. Dr. Jones was still there too. It seemed a long time to spend with one patient, and it also seemed to me that he was wasted on Bache.

Geoff picked me up at the Home at seven o'clock, in his well-polished grey saloon. He was still wearing the polo-necked sweater and sheepskin jacket that he wore on site, and he looked harassed. 'Sorry I haven't changed,' he said, 'but I'll have to go out to Church Vale estate before I can knock off. We've got trouble.'

I closed the door and pulled my skirt down. 'What sort of trouble?' I wished I had put on flatties instead of my new patent leather shoes.

'Flooding. Wouldn't you know? It's the blasted sewer in Charlecote Avenue. We've got the levels wrong somewhere. Dashed if I know how it happened, but there's all hell let loose. Residents' protest meetings, the lot. The City Surveyor's on our backs over it—I can't leave it till tomorrow. I'll have to go and calm the locals down, and the B.S.'ll expect a report in the morning too. *And* action.'

'You mean we've got to paddle about tonight?' I looked at my poor shoes again and wondered why he'd bothered to fetch me at all.

'You needn't. You can stay in the car, darling. Don't suppose it'll take long, then we'll go back to my place and I'll change my gear and take you for a meal or something. All right?'

It was all wrong, in fact, but it wasn't Geoff's fault. 'All right,' I said. 'It can't be helped.'

'No.' I felt him looking at me sidelong as we came to an open stretch of road. 'After all, I've had to hang around for you more than once, when *you've* come off late. Same thing.'

'That's different,' I said gently. 'That's always been because of the patients. They're not just inanimate bits of earthenware like sewers.'

'True. But use your loaf, darling. The people whose kitchens and gardens are three inches deep in filth aren't inanimate either. How would *you* like it?'

I was sorry then. 'Not much,' I confessed. 'Only it *doesn't* have the same degree of urgency as a—well, as an emergency for theatre, or somebody with pulmonary embolism, let's face it. Then it's a question of minutes, not hours.'

'Have it your own way. But there's one thing—if we don't get it right, and fast, you may have some emergency admissions with typhoid. See it that way.'

'We shan't. We don't take them any more. They'd have to go to City Isolation. Our Iso's a psychosomatic unit now.'

'A *whatter?*'

I explained.

'I see,' he said when I'd finished. 'Imaginary illnesses. That what you mean?'

'Oh, Geoff!' I wailed. '*No!* Really, you're as bad as the Fantail. She calls it the "faith-healing department". Those people are really *sick,* my dear.. They're not lead-swinging.'

'For example?'

'Well, there's a young student nurse. She gets the most frightful pain, and her pulse goes up ...' I told him about Bache as we drove on to Church Vale, and then I sat in the car and listened to a radio play while he splashed about in the front gardens of Charlecote Avenue, talking to angry men in shirt sleeves with bass brooms and shovels, and women in flowered overalls and Wellingtons. One of them shook her fist at him.

When he came back he slammed the door and sat biting his thumb before he started the engine. 'Hell,' he said at last. 'They're all talking about suing for damage to furniture and carpets. The old man'll just about go through the roof. It's that confounded Harris at the corner house who's stirred them all up. He's an expert little mixer. Well, can you wonder? *He's* the fellow who worked up that strike at the car-body factory. He's a professional agitator, that one.'

'You can't blame them,' I said. It wasn't very helpful of me, but it was true. 'You'd be good and mad if they were your carpets, wouldn't you? And I suppose they all got new ones to come to their new houses, and maybe they aren't even paid for. Or insured, either.'

He didn't say anything, but he started the car and drove carefully through the sludge until we came back to the main road. Then he said: 'Yes, it's high time we thought about some carpets of our own, isn't it? Darling, we ought to get down to thinking about a house. If only you'd change

27

your mind about not liking modern ones it would be simple. The old man'd just love to build one for us. I don't see why you're so mad keen for an old one.'

'I like a house to be cosy,' I said for the umpteenth time. 'And modern ones always look so bare and clinical somehow. Like outpatient consulting-rooms. And those ghastly picture windows all staring at one another instead of at a view. I just couldn't bear it. I want something cottagey—and besides, it'd be cheaper. Or Georgian, if you want to be grand ... Anyhow, I don't want to get married just yet. I haven't justified my existence as an S.R.N. yet. Geoff, you didn't even ask how I got on, on my first day of staffing.'

'Didn't I? Oh. Well, I had other things on my mind, you know. Sewers, for instance.'

Suddenly I was angry, and I was quite as surprised as he was. 'You always *will* have, won't you? All you want is a wife who'll be a background woman, and sit listening to a lot of stuff about storm drains, and soil-pipes, and J.C.B.s, and dumpy levels and things. It isn't even *interesting*! It doesn't have any human factor in it, until things go wrong and people wave their fists at you!'

'But of course it does. Houses and roads are built for *people*, aren't they?' He lifted his chin. 'Now don't be absurd, darling. You don't know what you're talking about.'

'Built for people? Oh no, they're not! They're built for a lot of statistics. You know, this man with two-point-three children, three-quarters of a car, and two hundred and fifty-three pounds in the Municipal Bank and about twenty in his current account, who reads the *Express*, smokes Senior Service, collects green stamps, and goes to the flicks seventeen and a half times a year. *People* indeed! They're just midgets. Manipulation fodder. All living in ticky-tacky boxes, and——'

'Now you've gone too far. Watch it! R.B.L. houses are *not* ticky-tacky.'

'Oh, yes they are!' I couldn't stop, once started. '*And* some of those awful flats, up by the hospital. In ten years' time they'll be scruffier than any Victorian tenement in Glasgow. That white stuff's going to be dark grey, for a start, and the lawns'll be covered with abandoned cars.'

'I see,' Geoff said between his teeth. 'If that's the way you feel I don't think it would be a very good idea for you to come on home with me. I mean, it wouldn't do to hand the old man that kind of talk. He wouldn't understand.'

Then I surprised myself again. I began to cry. 'I'm sorry,' I said. 'I'm tired, that's all. You'd better take me back, and I'll have an early night. It's been a bit of a day, changing wards and everything.'

There was one thing to be said for Geoff: his annoyance soon evaporated. 'Poor old girl. Got a headache, have you? All right. I'll take you straight back ... Be just as well, actually, because I shall have to go over all the sewer specifications with the old man, and it won't be much fun for you.'

He kissed me kindly outside the Home, and kept the engine running while I got out of the car. He was nearly out of sight when I reached the top of the steps.

Rose Innes was just coming out of the ground-floor changing room with her cape and her night case. She was pretty well my best friend, and I hadn't seen her all day because she'd been off, and she lived out. 'You look all pink and pleased,' I said. 'Did you *get* nights, then?'

She nodded. 'I did. *And* she sent Ratleigh to Geriatric to fit me in. She's foaming. What's more she practically promised me Humpherson's job when she goes. So I told Humph, and she said: "Then you won't have to wait long—we're moving the date forward to July." How about that, then?'

'Only four months,' I said. 'Scissors, that's soon to get your blues, isn't it? Still, you *are* the gold medallist.'

'Oh, don't rake *that* up!' Her fair skin was pinker than ever. 'Shall I never live it down? No, but haven't I been lucky? I hear you're on Iso. You're lucky too. It's gone all progressive down there, hasn't it?'

'Give me time,' I said. 'The plasterers haven't finished yet. But we have our little plans.'

She lifted one eyebrow. 'Who's "we"?'

'Oh, Sister Ross and me. And Caradoc Hughes. And maybe Dr. Ffestin-Jones. We'll let him have a say, probably.'

'That'll be nice for him! Crikey, I'd better float or I'll be late for night breakfast. See you in the morning, maybe?'

'Maybe,' I agreed. 'If I'm off.'

I had quite forgotten to look at the off-duty list before I left Isolation. That wasn't like me. I'd once forgotten when

I was young and green, and I'd gone on duty only to find that it was my day off, with breakfast in bed booked. Since then I'd always checked before I went off for the evening, because there were some ward sisters who were quite capable of altering the list without warning, in spite of what had been agreed with the Whitley Council. Not that I thought Sister Ross was one of them. And it wouldn't be my early morning off in any case, on a Tuesday. Staff nurses usually got them on Saturday or Sunday. That, and the extra holiday in the year, were about the only privileges we seemed to get if we lived in.

I shouldn't be living in much longer, I remembered. I'd promised to share Rose Innes's flat as soon as I got staffing pay, and that was only a fortnight away. Rose was a set ahead of me, and she'd moved out three months earlier, when she'd passed her hospital finals. Besides, she had a generous aunt who helped with the rent. It wasn't until I got to my room that I realised that there was something else I'd forgotten when I left Isolation, as well as my customary glance at the off-duty list. I'd been carrying my fob-watch loose in my pocket for days because the pin was shaky, and it wasn't in its usual place on the dressing-table with the rest of my pocket-paraphernalia. It was still, if nobody had moved it, on the thermometer shelf above Nurse Bache's bed. I was fond of that watch: it had been a present from Geoff, and I didn't want it mislaid.

There were two solutions, both illicit. I could ring through to Isolation and ask the senior night girl to lock it in the D.D.A. cupboard for me—and, even if the switchboard man would put me through, that might make trouble for Peters if Night Sister were to overhear what was strictly a personal call and therefore not allowed. Or I could break another rule by returning to the ward while off duty and in mufti, to fetch it. I decided to compromise. There was no law against mufti-clad nurses taking night walks in the grounds—though no doubt Miss Carte would regard it as a highly suspicious activity. And if my constitutional happened to take me near the block, and Peters happened to see me passing and chose to speak to me through the kitchen window—and even hand me my watch—she could scarcely be blamed for that. (The rules about off-duty communication with the wards were so strict that we often

30

wondered whether in the past people had been guilty of exhausting themselves with voluntary overtime, or whether such nameless orgies had gone on in ward kitchens o'nights that they had had to be stopped at all costs.)

I went downstairs by way of the fire-escape that led from the end of my corridor to the garden, and ran across the lawns to the block. It wasn't yet ten o'clock: Peters would be in the kitchen preparing hot drinks. If she wasn't I could hang around in the shrubbery until I saw her.

That was fine, as a theoretical plan. The trouble was that I hadn't bargained for the Home's high outside light being switched off, as it sometimes was during Home Sister's periodical fits of economy. Nor had it occurred to me that anyone else would be prowling about in the garden at the same time. So that when I tripped over a bush-root I had no hesitation in coming out with what a Victorian novel would term 'a rounded oath'—and it was a major shock to have a torch played on me where I lay.

'What on earth are you doing, crawling about there?' Sister Ross said.

Earth was the operative word. I got up silently and dusted most of it from my hands and knees, and then I said crossly, 'What do you think I'm doing, Sister? Keeping a romantic assignation with Dr. Ffestin-Jones, of course. We usually meet at the rabbit-hole by the second laurel, but I seem to have missed it.'

It was the first thing that came into my head. It was also pretty stupid of me not to realise that Theo Ross wasn't alone. The thin beam of a second throat-torch came at me straight away and walked up my arm to my face, and then both lights were snapped off. 'Oh, it's *you*, Staff!' Sister Ross said. She sounded breathless, as though she might be controlling a giggle. She had her girlish moments. 'Can you see now?'

I couldn't possibly go on to Isolation with her standing there. The watch would just have to take its chance. So I turned towards the Home again and headed carefully towards the dull glow from the Paisley-curtained sitting-room windows. 'Yes, thank you,' I said. 'I must have lost my sense of direction.'

Night Sister was coming out of the Home as I reached the door. It must have been her late night on, I suppose, because it was getting on for ten o'clock. She poked her head out of her hunched-up cape like a tortoise and said 'Good evening, Nairse,' and I said: 'Good evening, Miss Caudle,' and then she said it was dark without the outside light, wasn't it, and I remarked that it was a false economy because it had just cost me a pair of nylons in the shrubbery, and added: 'Oh, Sister, when you do a round in Isolation, *would* you be kind enough to ask Nurse Peters to look out for my watch? I left it on the shelf in Nurse Bache's cubicle, I think.'

'That was curless, Nairse,' she rebuked me. 'Very well. I'll *try* to remember.' She sighed, as though she had a two-thousand-bed multi-department hospital on her narrow shoulders, instead of the mere three hundred beds of Teddy's. 'And just be more curful with your things!'

'Yes, Sister,' I said.

She went scuttling on along the concrete walk, and I closed the door behind her and went up to bed. There was a note on my dressing-table, the corridor maid's unspeakable writing on the back of an old laundry list. It said *S. N. Jones. yuor fiansy Rung said you was not in yet. no Messadge left. Singed Flora.*

I sighed. I was not, repeat not, going all the way downstairs to the kiosk just to talk about sewers. I undressed rapidly, as though a nightdress would automatically insulate me from the things. As I brushed my hair I caught myself wondering who had been out in the shrubbery with Theo Ross. A man? And was it really possible to feel flirtatious just after parting with an impacted wisdom tooth? It seemed unlikely. Maybe she would explain in the morning.

I thought with pleasure, as I fell asleep, of the possibilities of the new régime in Isolation. It would be quite absurd to think about leaving Teddy's until I'd spent at least a couple of changes there. Geoff would simply have to get used to the idea, the way I'd accustomed myself to his sewer-passion. He was a fair person: he would just have to accept the fact that I too had my professional interests.

CHAPTER THREE

I met Rose coming the other way as I shot along the covered way to Iso next morning, and she put out one cloaked arm to check me. 'Hi,' she said. 'Listen, are you coming to live out or not? Because about a thousand other people are after me for a share of the flat, and——'

'Yes, of course I'm coming.' I frowned. 'Why did you think I mightn't?'

'Oh, I don't know. Geoff and whatnot, I suppose. And I'd so much rather have you than the others.'

'Damn Geoff!' I said. 'I've told him, I don't want to leave just yet. Hell, I haven't *been* a nurse yet, not effectively. Only the thing is that I won't have enough lolly till the end of the month, that's all.'

She let go my arm. 'Then that's O.K. Press on. I'll see you later, yes?'

'Sure,' I said. I hurried on, wondering why Rose, of all people, had suddenly turned out to be so career-minded, and setting out so determinedly in pursuit of her blues. I knew why I wanted to stay on; I knew—or thought I did— why Sister Ross had turned her back on domesticity. But Rose baffled me. She had been engaged twice during her training: once to a fifth-year who spent all his spare time prowling round the surgical side, and then failed his medicine finals and disappeared from our orbit; once to a bio-chemist—one of Dr. Sherwood's clever young men—who unaccountably walked out on her to marry a suspiciously bulgy physiotherapy girl. She had also, always, been able to take her pick of the available talent whenever there were dances or concerts where a girl needed an escort. She had generally given everyone—including me—the impression that once Registered she meant to shake the dust of Teddy's from her size three feet at the earliest opportunity and live the life of Riley for a time if not permanently. What was more, she was being fairly heavily pursued by Peter Ellis, who had once been Mr. Davidson's registrar and was now pretty close to a consultancy at Queen's, five miles away. She seemed to have settled down with Peter rather well, and certainly didn't encourage the hoi-polloi any more. There was nothing whatever in the way of a comfortable early marriage, if that was the object of the exercise, yet here she was chasing a junior night sister's job. And any staff nurse knows that that is the first step towards the petrifaction of institutionalised spinsterhood. Towards a pensionable career in Admin. Towards flat feet, irritating mannerisms, and the kind of voice that puts the fear of God into bewildered juniors. It wasn't Rose, to my mind. I meant to ask her about the Peter situation when I had time.

Iso was a wonderfully peaceful place first thing in the morning, by contrast with the scrabbling rush of every other ward I'd worked on. Even the departments had been fairly hectic: in Casualty and O.P. there were all the clinics to lay up, and an early scatter of queueing patients; in Theatre one simply never knew what to expect—it could be all hands on deck to set for an early list or an emergency, or the place could be in chaos after a busy night, with barely time for the daily wall-wash before we had to begin again. But down in Iso with its cubicled layout nobody was visibly hurrying, and Peters, the night senior, was pouring tea in the kitchen while the two third-years read the report through.

I looked at the duty list first: I was on until four, and Caradoc was due on at two. Sister Ross wasn't due until after first lunch, either, which left me in charge. So I said, 'What, tea at this hour? Is this the done thing down here?'

Peters nodded and shoved a saucerless cup towards me. 'Oh, yes. Even when Sister's on. Her idea, actually. She doesn't like disturbing these patients too early, she says. It's as good an excuse as any, I suppose. Anyway, I can give you the report while we drink it just as easily as if we went dry. Oh, your watch wasn't in Bache's cubicle, by the way. And she said she didn't remember seeing it. I can't find it anywhere else, either.'

'Damn,' I said. 'I was sure I'd——'

'But maybe Caradoc picked it up. He was in there after you, perhaps.'

'Yes, maybe he did.' I hoped he had. It was part of me, part of my training, and I didn't particularly want to lose it. Geoff had given it to me when I signed on, after P.T.S. We hadn't been engaged then, and I'd thought it rather generous of him—especially in view of the fact that he'd thoroughly disapproved of the whole project. Nursing, he felt, was a rather messy business. Not quite the class of thing for the future wife of an eminent civil engineer. Not that he was anywhere near eminence, but he certainly meant to end up in the Telford class if he could. He was coldly ambitious about that: today Bright, Richards, and Lockyer; tomorrow the world, as Rose had once put it. Rose didn't much like Geoff, she said he wasn't human enough. Maybe that was because he saw her as 'too light-hearted for a nurse'. It never occurred to him that she was rather better at wearing a protective shell than I was.

In Geoff's view it would have been far more ladylike if I had taken a good secretarial course, combined with a little *cordon bleu* cookery and a suitable amount of deportment and social know-how, at one of those disgracefully expensive establishments that cater for minor princesses and the unacademic daughters of tycoons. That was probably his mother's angle: she had originally been his father's secretary and regarded nurses as 'rather common'. Geoff and I had our first squabble about that: I told him that any nitwit could learn shorthand and typing, and he retorted that to have to look after 'just any sort of person' would be degrading. I think he was pretty sure that I'd chuck the whole thing up inside three months—but when I didn't he gave me the watch as a sort of peace-offering, and I'd worn and used it ever since.

'I don't think much of Stanway,' Peters was saying. 'She doesn't sleep, you know. She had two lots of sodium amytal last night, again, and for all the effect it had I might as well give her banana sandwiches.'

'She's worried,' I said. 'And I don't blame her, either. Heck, *I'd* worry. Wouldn't you? ... What about the Sugden boy?'

'His temp's down a bit, but he's awfully chesty. Still, I suppose they'll be giving him nitrogen–mustard again. Poor kid. He was fifteen when this began, you know. Diagnosed at sixteen. I don't know on earth he's come so far. He *can't* go much longer. Five years . . . It's a hell of a time.'

I knew all about the leukaemias, the same as she did, but I shook my head. 'Don't say that, Peters. You don't *know*. They might——'

'Find a cure? I've heard that one before. That's what his parents keep saying, poor loves. But I've a nasty feeling in my bones that it won't happen. Not in time for Tony, any-way . . . All the others are comfortable. Rutherford and Hillman are really ready for discharge, if the S.S.O. looks in, I should think.'

'*Will* he look in?'

'You must be joking!' Peters put down her empty cup and widened her eyes at me. 'I thought everybody knew.'

'Knew what?'

'Why, about him and Theo Ross. Come on, you haven't been on nights or anything.'

'Really? But I thought—well, she told me——'

'About the one that got away? Maybe, but that doesn't mean she's hung up her—what did Diana use? Arrows, or a spear?—her weapons for good. Oh, I know she gives every-one this dedicated bit, but believe you me, there's life in the old dog yet, mate.'

'She's very attractive,' I said. I was curiously relieved, and couldn't think why, that Sister Ross was reputed to be involved with the S.S.O. Mr. Verrier was a nice man, a widower in his early forties, with a dry sense of humour that none of us really understood. 'He's too clever for me,' I said. 'I'm sure more than half his jokes go over my head. But he's great to work with in theatre, I'll say that for him. He never flaps. Not like dear Mr. Davidson. That man——!'

'What man?' Nancy Serpell said at the door. 'If you mean Dr. Jones, be careful. These walls have ears, and there are those among us who see him as the *Roi Soleil* of Iso . . . Will you take a look at Stanway when you do your round? She's a mite too drowsy for my liking. Slurred, too.'

'I will,' I promised. 'When I've looked at Tony Sugden. And if she hasn't slept she's likely to be, by now.'

I slipped on a barrier-nursing gown outside Tony's room

before I went in, and pulled my mask up. He was propped up on a bed-rest, and his face was flushed as well as tanned. It made him look too well to have such a thin little hold on life. He was the least bit moon-faced from having steroids, but only a professional eye would have noticed it. He managed to smile, too. He had beautiful teeth: they reminded me of Dr. Jones's. 'And good morning to you,' I said. 'I hear that you're a bit wheezy today. By the way, I'm Nurse Jones.'

'*Staff* Nurse Jones,' he corrected me.

'Well, yes. But I'm not used to it yet.' I noticed the length of his thick dark lashes. They were such a waste, I thought. Then I told myself not to be defeatist. Hadn't I just grumbled at Peters for that very thing? 'Yes, you do sound a bit bubbly.'

'Just a bit,' he said. 'Not the—the first time. I suppose I'll have those awful injections again?'

'I don't know, love. That's for Dr. Watterson to decide. You've seen Dr. Hastri, haven't you? I expect Dr. Watterson will be in this morning. Anyhow, if they do you good . . .' I didn't know what to say to him.

'Oh, I'm not grumbling,' he said quickly. 'Everyone's been marvellous to me here, every time I've been in. I know they do their best.'

'But it gets tedious? I know. Well now, what can we do to cheer you up? Would you like something to read, or radio, or company?'

'Radio, please. I never get tired of music.'

I put my hand up to reach the headphones from the shelf above his bed, but he said: 'No, these are a bit tiring to wear.' I ought to have thought of that myself. 'I've got my own transistor set here somewhere. Maybe it's in the locker.'

I got it out for him and put it close to him on the bed-table. 'It's a jolly nice one. Hacker? They're very well thought of, aren't they?' Geoff had one, I remembered. Nothing but the best did for him.

'Yes. I saved up for it for months. It helps to—to make the time go by when I have a bad spell. I was so well last week. I went to a motor-cycle scramble.'

'You rode in it?'

'No, not this time. But I rode *to* it.'

'Good for you,' I said. 'Let's hope it isn't long before you can compete again.'

He didn't say anything. He was used to that sort of bromide, I suppose. I'd been stupid to offer it: his look told me that he knew exactly what the score was, and I felt about two centimetres high.

I turned away awkwardly and closed the door behind me. Nancy Serpell was just coming out of Stanway's room. 'Oh, there you are,' she said. 'Stanway's asleep now.' She was frowning.

'But what? You don't like the look of her?'

She shook her head. 'I don't know. See what you think.'

I was in there about seventeen seconds flat. Just long enough to check her pupils, try to find her pulse, and hear one slow stertorous breath. 'Get First On,' I told Serpell, 'and then give me a hand.'

I darted into the sterilising room and assembled funnel, tubing, Ryle's tube and jug on a tray. Serpell caught up a bucket on her way back from the phone and trotted after me. 'Tummy washout?' she asked.

'Yes. I'm taking no chances. No wonder the sodium amytal didn't work. She must have——' I stopped. It wasn't fair to assume anything. I didn't really know.

Serpell wasn't so particular. 'Hoarded it, you mean? Oh lord!'

'I could be wrong,' I said, when I'd managed to get the Ryle's tube in and the first funnelful was flowing. 'I'm using saline, by the way, not soda bic. There's a theory that it's a good thing when it's barbiturates. Makes 'em sick, too, I dare say.'

'Or combines with the sodium?'

'Shouldn't think so. Look, it *could* be a pressure thing, but if it is this won't do any harm. I daren't risk waiting till First On gets here. Who's on, anyway?'

'Miss Greene from Cas, I expect, at this hour. They usually cover for residents' breakfast, don't they? So nice to have breakfast at a civilised hour, when the world's aired a bit. Yes, it'll be Miss Greene.'

'It *would* be.' I had no great opinion of Miriam Greene. She was a ditherer. I turned the funnel down over the bucket. 'Look at that—I was right. Bits of blue capsules, and a whole one.' I refilled the funnel and held it up high again, letting the warm saline run in fast. 'Now remember, not a word outside this ward, Serpell.'

'Of course not!' She was hurt by the suggestion, I think, but I had to say it. It was routine. 'Think she'll do?'

'Yes.' I turned the funnel down when I'd run another pint in. 'Look, most of them are undissolved.'

'You can't blame her.' Serpell sounded anxious, as if she was expecting me to preach a sermon about it.

I looked up. 'I'm not. I'm just kicking myself. We ought to have foreseen it. Peters ought to have watched her take the stuff; I ought to have looked at her before I went to Tony.'

'And *I* ought to have realised how deep she was! But I didn't go right in when I saw she was asleep.'

'That's understandable. No, what I mean is that when nurses are patients, they should be treated as patients. We shouldn't take so much for granted. They're only people, after all. If any other patient had made up her mind she'd got sarcoma, and got depressed about it, we should have taken all the proper precautions. If we had, this wouldn't have happened. She wouldn't have had the chance to——Look round her gear, Serpell.'

While I went on with the lavage Serpell searched the locker, the pillows, and all the pockets she could find. 'Two,' she said. 'In her sponge-bag.' She passed me the two capsules and I slipped them into my pocket.

Then Peters, returned by some hunch from night nurses' dinner, put her head in. 'I had a feeling,' she said, when she had taken in the set-up. 'If you're wondering—which is what I've been doing all through dinner—the most she can have collected is forty-three sixty-milligram capsules.' She was pale. 'Oh, God, *why* didn't I watch her take the blasted things?'

'Forty-one,' I said. 'We've just found two.' I could—and probably should—have said: 'Why didn't you?' but Peters had got the message without any reproaches from me. 'See anyone coming down?'

'Yes, the Greene female's at the other end of the walk, coming this way. Did you ring?'

'You'd better scarper before she comes,' I said.

Stanway opened her eyes as I slid the Ryle's tube out, and

coughed. I hid the funnel behind me and swabbed her face. 'All right? Just relax, old dear. You'll feel better in a sec.'

She licked her lips and drew in a deep gurgling breath. Then she murmured: 'You shouldn't . . .' and closed her eyes again.

I gathered up the trayful of stuff and managed to dump it in the sluice-room in time to meet Miss Greene at the door. 'What's all this?' she wanted to know. 'Nurse said somebody was *comatose*. You haven't anyone down here that——'

'A sick nurse,' I explained. 'Query new growth of skull.'

'But if she's comatose surely the S.S.O. should——'

'She isn't now,' I said briskly. 'In fact you don't really need to see her at all, Miss Greene.'

'Staff Nurse, you didn't send for me for nothing, I'm quite sure. Of course I must look at her. Which is her room?'

I had to tell her the rest then, though I didn't want to. I said it as quietly as I could, because, as Serpell had already remarked, the hardboard cubicle walls had ears. 'An overdose,' I mouthed. 'Sodium amytal.'

'But how did she *get* it, Staff Nurse?' Miss Greene's eyes were positively beady. She was a great one for catching out the nursing staff whenever she could.

'We'll have to sort that out later,' I said. 'When Sister comes on. If you'll just check her condition for me . . .'

'Her own doctor ought to see her as soon as possible. I mean, in the circumstances he may want Dr. Jones to see her too.'

'Yes, Miss Greene. I certainly don't want the responsibility.'

I stood by while she checked Stanway's reflexes. She was very meticulous about it. It was a neurological examination according to *Clinical Methods*, Chapter Nine, as far as it went, which is to say in the absence of any electrical apparatus. Stanway was conscious, pretty well, but she didn't say anything and neither did Miss Greene until she had finished and we were outside again. Then she gave me a disapproving look. 'I'll have to *report* this, you know. It's a very serious matter.'

'Of course,' I said. 'As long as you don't put anything in her notes. I'll be telling the S.S.O. myself, and I'll explain to

Sister when she comes on. Then it's up to them.'

'Yes, it must definitely be reported. It's a very strict rule, Staff Nurse.'

If it was, it was one I had never heard of. But I simply said: 'Yes, Miss Greene.' When I had got her to the ward door I said: 'Any treatment?'

'No, not if the S.S.O. is to see her. Just give her some coffee, please. I expect that will be welcome, after a stomach washout. You did *give* her one?'

'Of course!'

'It's not "of course" at all, Staff Nurse. You really ought to have waited for instructions, you know.'

That, I reflected, would have been a fat lot of good.

Serpell, who had been hovering, was already making the coffee, so I left her to it and got on with my round of the other patients. I'd done the charting, and sent Serpell and Robson off to the canteen for their elevenses before I went back to Stanway. Before I could reach her door the phone rang, and I turned back to the office to answer it. It was Geoff. 'You shouldn't ring me *here*,' I said straight away. 'Geoff, I'm on duty. I can't——'

'Well, the switchboard put me through,' he said. 'I only wanted to ask what time you're off duty, that's all. It doesn't take a minute.'

At that point Dr. Ffestin-Jones walked in, smiled amiably and sat on Sister's desk to wait. 'I can't talk now,' I said hurriedly. 'I can't see you today, anyway.' I put the receiver down with a little bang. 'I'm sorry, Dr. Jones.'

'For what?'

'Keeping you waiting, sir,' I said.

He looked down at something in the palm of his hand. 'Only about five seconds,' he qualified. Then he was swinging my watch between his finger and thumb. He had beautifully shaped nails, I noticed. 'Yours, by any chance?'

'I thought I'd lost it!' I held out my hand and he dropped the watch into my palm, warm from his pocket. 'Did you——?'

'I used it for Nurse Bache to focus on.' He saw that I was puzzled, smiled, and added: 'Hypnosis-wise ... Then I pocketed it without thinking. "To Delia, with love from Geoffrey." So you're a Delia?'

41

My face was already hot, and when he said my name, twice, in that soft lilting voice of his, it must have been scarlet. 'Nobody *calls* me that,' I said. 'It's usually Didi. For "D.D." you see.'

'But "Delia" is lovely. What a pity not to use it.' He got off the desk and stood up. He was a lot taller than I was. 'Still, I'm in the same boat. Nobody ever calls me "Dwyryd", either. It's usually "Dwy" at most. Do you know what "Dwyryd" means?'

I thought of what few Welsh words I knew. 'Two— something?'

'Two fords, originally. From *dwy* and *rhyd*. Actually, it's the name of a river. A rather good salmon river. I was born on its banks, so to speak.'

He seemed ready to go on talking indefinitely, and I might have let him if I hadn't been worried. He was easy to listen to. 'I see,' I said. 'Dr. Jones, is Nurse Stanway in any way a patient of yours? Or is she purely a sick nurse under the S.S.O.?'

'I've talked to her in passing, that's all.' He was alert at once. 'You worried about her?'

'I don't know whether I ought to——' It was difficult.

'All right. In confidence.'

'I don't know whether you know, but she's got it into her head that she's malignant. There's this lump on her head— they've done a biopsy, but the report isn't through yet. She's convinced herself that it's a sarcoma, and that she needs a high protein anti-cancer diet, and so on ... Well, this morning she took an overdose of sodium amytal. She must have hoarded it. She's all right now—I gave her a tummy washout, and Miss Greene's looked at her—but she'll still be depressed, and it might be a good idea for you to talk to her. Only I can't ask you to, if she's not your patient.'

'I see. Who else knows? About the ... episode.'

That made me smile. Psychiatrists have a reputation for using that word 'episode' for almost any kind of anti-social behaviour, from multiple murder downwards. 'Nurse Serpell, Nurse Peters, Miss Greene.'

'Miss Greene?' His eyebrows went up towards his dark hair. I don't think he had much opinion of her either. 'Well, you deal with your nurses, and I'll handle Miss Greene. We don't want the grapevine to play about with it, do we?'

'I've already warned them not to talk,' I said. 'But they wouldn't, anyway. A patient, they might, but a nurse, no.'

'Good. I'll just make a couple of phone calls, and then I'll have a word with her. All right?'

I went out of the office while he talked. Psychiatrists are the only doctors in hospital whose phone calls are considered private, and the only ones who can legitimately be left unchaperoned with a female patient. They have a nice life, compared with the others. When he came out looking for me I took him to Stanway and left him to get on with it.

By the time he came out of her room I'd got through a fair amount of the paper-work that was waiting for me and answered several enquiries from relatives. I had just put the receiver down after telling Tony Sugden's people they could visit during the evening when he put his head in at the office door. 'She won't do anything like that again,' he told me.

I stood up. 'You're sure?'

'No need to.' He smiled. 'The path. lab. say that the biopsy showed no signs of malignancy. The S.S.O. says that in that case it's a cyst for removal and he'll do it as soon as he can fix it. So no lunch for her, pending hearing from him.'

'Jolly good,' I said. 'Now, Nurse Bache *is* yours, I think, isn't she?' I was so relieved about Stanway that I found myself smiling back at him.

'She is. What do you make of her?'

'Well, I *suppose* she's a hysteria. Only I don't see what she has to gain. If she wants to leave, why doesn't she? And besides . . .'

'The symptoms are almost too convincing?'

'Something like that, yes.'

'They can be, you know. Very dramatic at times . . . There's some trouble at home, I rather think.'

'She came here to get away, you mean? And now she can't face this, either, so she's retreated into illness?'

His teeth glinted. They were extraordinarily white. 'I see you've read all the right books. Yes, but that's an over-simplification, of course. It's roughly how it works. Only I

43

don't know yet what the unfaceable is at home.'

He went on looking at me, and I got the message. 'So you want *me* to find out?'

'Nothing as deliberate as that, no. No probing—that would be fatal. But she might talk. If she does . . . well . . .'

'It's a bit like spying, isn't it? I mean, here we are, with it well drummed into us to regard patients' confidences as more or less sacred—and then you come along and want it all repeated to you.'

He sighed, and came to sit on the corner of the desk. He was wearing a Bangor University tie, like little Dr. Evans's. 'Look, you wouldn't fail to report glycosuria to a physician, would you? Or secondary haemorrhage to a surgeon? And you wouldn't think of hiding the temperature charts on rounds day.'

'Well, no,' I agreed. 'But it isn't quite the same.'

'It's *exactly* the same. Psychiatric illness *is* an illness, like any other. If patients are mentally ill, then it's up to you to report what appears to go on in their minds. Yes?'

I frowned at him. 'You can't call little Bache "mentally ill",' I objected. 'I mean, she isn't *insane* in any way.'

Evidently he had covered this ground before. He folded his hands on his knees and leaned forwards. Then he took a deep breath. 'Listen. I used to be a registrar in a big psychiatric hospital. Fourteen hundred beds. *All* those people were mentally ill—but only about fifty would be what you'd call insane. When I say "insane" I mean far enough out of touch with reality to need to be in locked wards, for their own protection and for the protection of others. You don't have to be raving mad to be mentally ill, Delia.'

I had never before been addressed by my Christian name by anyone over the rank of houseman. It was disconcerting, and I think I was blushing again. 'I don't know much about it,' I confessed. 'We don't get many psychology lectures, and none of us has a clue about psychiatry. I mean, we know that you come in and see people—but they're always someone else's patients too. We ought to have a proper psychiatric unit. You'll have to teach me.'

'I mean to,' he said. 'Teach you, *and* get a proper unit going.'

He wandered off into Bache's room then, and I went along to Stanway. She was trotting about in her dressing

44

gown, and announced that when she felt less groggy she might be able to help with the teas.

When Dr. Watterson came down to give Tony his nitro-mustard injection I let Robson go with him. I told myself that it was because she had never seen them given, but that wasn't true: in fact I knew how painful they were, and I didn't much want to be in on it. Eventually the S.S.O. came down. He discharged both the appendicectomy girls, and then spent five minutes chatting to Stanway and five more making up her notes. He didn't mention the 'episode', but he asked for her to go up to theatre at six o'clock. 'We'll have finished Mr. Davidson's list by five,' he said.

'Yes,' I said. 'I'll tell Sister. She'll be on this evening. Any special prepping?'

'No, just a straight shave, please, Staff.' He looked up from his notes. 'Missing Ward Five?'

I tried not to look too overjoyed. 'Not a bit.' I would have liked to tell him that it was no hardship to be away from Miss Fantague, but I didn't know him well enough. 'I think it will be very interesting down here.'

He looked doubtful. 'Personally, I like to deal with things I can see. Seems to me that physicians have far too much guesswork, as it is, and as for psychiatry—well, it's *all* a matter of conjecture, isn't it? Or have you already fallen under the spell of the Celtic twilight?'

I didn't know quite how to take that—I never did know how to take the S.S.O.—but I said: 'I'm open-minded, Mr. Verrier.'

He grinned as he got up. 'Tell me that in a month's time, Staff.'

On my way to lunch I stopped at the kiosk in the main entrance and rang Geoff, at head office. 'Sorry if I bit your head off,' I apologised. 'I was just busy when you rang, and I had Dr. Jones standing there, and——'

'I only wanted to ask you to come and look at a house with me this evening,' he explained. 'But I've put them off now, and by tomorrow it'll be gone. It's no good hanging about at this game—you have to be quick off the mark, you know.'

'What's the hurry?' I said. 'We don't need it *yet*.'

'We'll never get one if you keep saying that, Didi. Now,

which nights *are* you free? In case something else crops up.'

Quite suddenly the very last thing on earth that I wanted to do was to inspect houses with Geoff. It all sounded so horribly final. I panicked and began to make excuses. 'Well, I don't know. I've got to move into this flat, for one thing. With Rose, you know. And——'

'But why move into a flat? Where's the point? You'll be leaving there soon, in any case.'

'But I promised Rose, Geoff! I mean, she can't manage all the rent by herself.' That was a blatant lie: I didn't remember ever feeling I had to lie to Geoff before, and I didn't think much of it. 'At least, she can because her aunt helps her. But she doesn't want to sponge if she needn't. She does *want* to get a flatmate.'

'Maybe, but it doesn't have to be *you*,' Geoff said. I could hear the possessive note in his voice again. 'Surely she has other friends? And if she hasn't, then there must be something wrong with her.' He sounded more like a heavy father than a fiancé.

'Well, we'll talk about it,' I said obstinately. 'I'll ring you.'

It was curry for lunch, and I couldn't manage more than half of mine. I seemed to have totally lost my appetite. I would have to see Rose, I reminded myself, and arrange to move in, if only so that I wouldn't have told Geoff fibs after all. Besides, I told myself, it would be to Geoff's advantage for me to move out. With Rose on nights, we should have the flat to ourselves when I came off duty in the evenings. That would mean fewer visits to his home and less opportunity for his mother to get at me about leaving Teddy's. It would also be cheaper—we had long ago reached the stage of going shares in most of our outings. Not that Geoff was short of money—he did very nicely out of the firm—but it was something he felt engaged couples ought to do. That was probably one of his mother's ideas, too.

I took one look at the chocolate mousse and decided to live without it. While I was drinking my coffee Matron's secretary came into the dining-room, hunting someone, and finally squirmed her way round to me. 'Can you see Matron at two-thirty?' she wanted to know. 'Don't ask me what it's about, because I don't know.'

46

I felt cold. Everybody feels cold when Matron sends a summons, especially when it's out of regular nurse-seeing time. 'I'll be there,' I said. I drank another cup of coffee before I went back to Iso.

CHAPTER FOUR

'You'd better have a quick cuppa before you go, then,' Sister Ross said. She looked at me in an amused kind of way. 'What on earth have you been up to? You look positively furtive.'

I shrugged, warming the teapot at the hot tap. 'I don't know. Whenever Matron sends for me all my past life rises up, as it were, and there are so many things . . . It could be holidays, P.A.Y.E. coding, anything. But I always feel guilty when I walk in.'

'Me, too,' she admitted. 'Oh, you needn't look so surprised! A navy blue dress is no protection. Heavens, I've even seen Home Sister creeping out of there in tears.'

That did shake me. 'Miss *Pipe?* But she's——'

'Years older than Matron, and as tough as they come? Yes, but it doesn't help, you know.'

I poured two cups of tea: I was rapidly learning that the pot never had time to cool down in Iso. 'It's like being sent for by the Head, at school. I practically went down with gastro-enteritis every time . . . I'd better tell you all the details when I get back, Sister, but quite a few things happened this morning. The S.S.O.'s discharged Hillman and Rutherford. Dr. Watterson's given Tony his nitrogen–mustard. Dr. Jones looked at Bache, and——' I hesitated, looking up at the clock. 'I'll have to *go*, Sister.' There was no point in embarking on the Stanway saga and having to abandon it.

'Trot on, then.' She was leafing through the S.S.O.'s notes on the desk. 'I see Stanway's for theatre today?'

I nodded. 'Yes. I'll tell you the rest when I get back. Just a straight shave, he said, no prep.' Evidently there was nothing in the notes about the 'episode'—I had never thought there would be—but I should have to report it verbally, nevertheless. There was no question about that.

For once Miss Carte wasn't scratching away with her pen when I walked in. She fixed her eyes on me as soon as I closed the door behind me, and I swear she didn't blink for a full minute. I don't think I did, either: I felt quite paralytic. After a while the saliva began to flow again and I got out: 'You wanted to see me, Matron?'

She hunched her head into her shoulders like a tortoise and her glasses became an eyeless glitter. There was one long grey hair swinging from the brim of her frilled cap: there must have been an atrocious draught from somewhere. 'Miss Jones——' That was bad. Very bad. It would have been a fairly ominous indicator if she'd called me 'Nurse' instead of 'Staff Nurse', but 'Miss Jones' was several stages worse. I wondered whether she ever called Sister 'Miss Ross', and if so what for. What *could* a ward sister do that was so terrible, short of actually murdering a patient, or seducing the S.M.O., or selling the ward supply of hard drugs in the local coffee bar? 'Miss Jones,' she was saying, 'you sent a uniform dress to the laundry this morning?'

That threw me completely. I had half expected a lot of things, but nothing as innocent as that. 'Yes, Matron.' I began to relax.

'And what else?'

I frowned, thinking back. I had rushed over to my room to change when I'd got around to my canteen break. After Dr. Jones and before Dr. Watterson, I remembered. 'Eight aprons,' I said. Our caps, collars, and cuffs were all disposable, so there couldn't have been much else. 'Oh, and a sheet and pillowcase, of course.'

'*And?*'

I couldn't imagine what she was after. It was an odd sort of question, and I didn't see where it was leading. 'Nothing else, Matron.'

Her hand came out and spilled two bright blue capsules on to her big empty blotter. 'What about these, Miss Jones?'

I could have kicked myself. When I had dragged on my clean dress and pushed the used one into the laundry hamper I had automatically plucked out my pen and torch, and retrieved my long chain of safety-pins and my scissors. But I had forgotten all about the capsules at the bottom of my empty watch-pocket. I rarely used that pocket. We all wore our fob-watches pinned on our aprons: the standard watch-pocket in our dresses was useful only for the kind of patient-bestowed sweets—unwrapped, or from unsavoury characters—that one meant to jettison in the kitchen waste-bin. I stared at the blue capsules and tried to compose a suitable reply.

'Well, Miss Jones?' Matron waited. 'Were they pre-scribed for you by the S.M.O.?'

I only wished they had been. 'No, Matron.'

'Then you took them from your ward supply?'

'No—well, not exactly, Matron. I meant to put them back in the cupboard . . .' I tailed off into silence.

'I think you'd better elaborate, Miss Jones. Being in pos-session of dangerous drugs is a very serious matter. Or doesn't that occur to you?'

I would hardly have termed a hundred and twenty milli-grams of sodium amytal 'dangerous drugs' myself, but she was dead right about the fact that I'd put myself hopelessly in the wrong by taking the wretched things away with me. There was no help for it: I had to tell her the whole story, damping it down where I could.

When I had finished she sat back. 'Yes. Exactly. Now, why was not all this reported to me earlier? You know perfectly well that such a—a *demonstration* in the case of a member of the nursing staff should be reported to my office instantly, night or day. Don't you?'

'Demonstration' was Matronese for the psychiatric 'epi-sode', I supposed. And I hadn't, in fact, thought about the usual Admin rule that all cases of serious staff illness must be reported to Matron's office on the spot. I hadn't seen it as 'illness'. I told her so. 'It wasn't as though she'd suddenly been struck down with anything serious, Matron.'

'No? Miss Greene thought it serious, Miss Jones, if you didn't. It could have been *fatal*!'

So she *had* reported it. I might have known. But I suppose I had trusted Dr. Jones to silence her. He had probably been too late.

'I had intended to send for you and Nurse Peters in any case,' she went on. 'But when Laundress brought these to me at lunch-time it seemed to me that there was dangerous slackness—slackness *and* disobedience—going on in Isolation. You have discussed the matter with Sister Ross, of course?'

'Not—not yet, Matron. I haven't had time.'

'Not *time*? You've had half an hour, Nurse.'

That 'Nurse' must have slipped out unintentionally, but I felt we were now past the worst. After all, what could she do to me? It was all so petty. She couldn't take away my privilege of holding the drug keys, now that I was State Registered. Or could she?

She must have been psychic, because she immediately launched into a spiel about how she could prevent my holding the keys, and what a disgrace it would be to have to reorganise all the off-duty so that only Caradoc or Sister was ever left in charge. Only she wasn't going to. She thought it would already have been a salutary lesson to me. It then transpired that it was Peters who was due for the real rocket. Such incredible slackness in a senior night nurse was not to be tolerated: Nurse Peters was being transferred to days, where she would receive adequate supervision. And more in the same vein. 'So, Staff Nurse'—at least we were back to normal protocol—'you will now go off duty, and report for night duty at ten o'clock. Staff Nurse Innes will cover for you until then.'

There was just one thing ... 'You mean, in Isolation, do you, Matron?'

'But of course! To replace Nurse Peters. Very well, off you go.'

'I'll have to go back and finish giving Sister Ross the report first, Matron,' I mentioned. 'About Nurse Stanway, and——'

She glanced at the nasty little chromium clock on her desk. 'Very well. And you go off immediately after that. And Staff Nurse——'

'Yes, Matron?'

'Let me have no more slackness, please. If I receive any more complaints of your behaviour I shall have to consider very seriously whether you are suitable for staff nurse's duties at all.'

If that was meant to strike dread into my heart, it did. I reached out towards the capsules on the blotter. 'Shall I take those back, Matron?'

It would not have surprised me if she had felt I wasn't capable of carrying them back without having an orgy on the way, but she only frowned and wrapped them in a clean requisition slip from her stationery rack. 'See that they are returned *at once* to the drug cupboard, Staff Nurse.' Anyone would think she was handing over a nuclear warhead, at the very least.

Now that it was over, my brain began to tick normally again. It occurred to me that I might as well kill two birds while I was about it, rather than come back next day. 'Matron, I've been meaning to come and see you ... I'd like permission to live out.'

She looked up. I fancied she was relieved, as well she might be with such a shortage of staff accommodation that there was talk of taking over the Residency for nursing staff. 'Where are you proposing to live?'

'With Staff Nurse Innes, Matron. She's offered me a share of her flat, in Guerdon Road.'

Guerdon Road was respectable enough. She nodded. 'You'll have a bedroom to yourself?'

'Oh yes, Matron.'

'You know that I don't approve of sharing rooms, or beds?'

I did. I also knew that at least six people had been made to return to the Home because the Ass. Mat. she sent to inspect our lodgings discovered that they were sleeping in double beds. Matron had a thing about double beds: we were not quite sure whether she thought we might invite our boy-friends to share them, or whether she suspected us of even worse activities. But, as Rose had said when Miss Brewer called at 53 Guerdon Road, 'Hell, if we wanted to sin, a single bed wouldn't throw us, would it?'

'Permission granted,' Matron said. She dragged her scribbling pad towards her. 'I'd like the date of your proposed removal, so that I can get your board and lodging payments refunded.'

Pay and emoluments, though paid out monthly, were made up to Thursday nights, I knew. So I said: 'I thought Friday might be convenient.'

'Very well. You may leave a note with my secretary if there is any change of plan.'

I didn't imagine there would be. Rose wouldn't really worry if she had to wait for part of the rent.

When I got back to the ward Sister was waiting for me at the office door. Matron had already rung her, I gathered. 'So you're off to nights?' she said. 'No sooner do I get a team together than it's broken up.'

'But I'll be *here*,' I said. 'And you'll have Peters on days in my place, presumably.' It was a change to have a ward sister actively not wanting to lose me, which just showed how different Theo Ross was from most of her colleagues. Nurses sometimes like, often sincerely admire, ward sisters; it's almost unheard-of for a sister to express a preference for a specific nurse. But perhaps, I thought, this was something that applied only to staff nurses? I wasn't yet used to being one.

Evidently Matron had said no more, because Sister Ross was still looking baffled. 'But *why* is she swopping you over?'

'Didn't she tell you, Sister?'

'Would I ask if she had? No, she just said you were to go off and report for nights.'

When I'd finished enlightening her she said: 'Peters is a perfect fool! As for Stanway, I won't say one word to her unless she brings it up herself, poor lamb. And *you* were careless—but at least you had the sense to give first-aid.'

I handed over the capsules. 'I suppose these should go back into stock. It'll make you two surplus, because they'd already been booked out. And they've been pretty well handled by now—so shall I burn them?'

'Yes,' she said. And then: 'No! We can't waste expensive stuff like that. You can have them: you may need them if you're to get any sleep today.'

I opened my eyes at that little bit of irregularity. 'I don't know what Matron would say, Sister!'

She smiled. 'Neither do I. And frankly, Jones, I don't damn well care. Off you go, if you've nothing more to confess.'

When I was reaching down my cape I said: 'Sorry to leave you in the lurch with the teas and things. But Caradoc will be on all day now, and you'll have Mrs. Doherty till six, and the Hodder girl afterwards, as well as Robson.'

'Meaning that I'm incapable of handling a few teas without at least three people to help me? I have *been* a junior, you know! By the way, there are one or two admissions coming this afternoon. No idea what. You'll find out when you come on.'

'Yes. I'm not on till ten,' I mentioned. 'Rose Innes will cover.'

'Well, so long as I have somebody sensible.' She looked up at the indicator lights as someone's buzzer sounded. It was Bache's. 'Here we go,' she said. 'There are times when I could spank that child. Hard.'

I left her talking to Bache with infinite gentleness.

I slept in my own room. There was no point in moving three floors to the night quarters if I was going out altogether in two days' time. It was going to work out even better when I was on nights, I reflected, now that Rose was on nights too. Matron didn't know it, but she had succeeded in doing me a good turn. I'd always preferred nights: the sound and smell, and intimate atmosphere, of a hospital at night is quite unlike its daylight climate. Even people were different, less superficial.

Then I considered Geoff's probable reactions. He was not going to be pleased. When I was off duty he would be striding about muddy building sites, or sitting in the draughty site-office of the B.R.L. roadworks project. And when he was free I should be going on duty. Certainly I couldn't make any firm dates with him until I knew when my nights-off were due. We had ten nights free in four weeks—but not necessarily *en bloc*—and I might have to wait three weeks to get them.

As I took the short cut through the shrubbery to go on duty I was plotting to ask Miss Caudle whether Rose and I might sometimes be off simultaneously: nothing is more annoying, on nights-off, than having to tiptoe about while one's flat-mate sleeps. And then somebody flashed a torch-beam quickly across my apron-bib badges. Remembering my previous encounter I said: 'Is that you, Sister Ross?'

'Nothing so feminine.' I heard a soft laugh before I saw that it wasn't. Dr. Jones touched my elbow. 'Only me, Delia.'

'Oh, it's you?' I wondered whether he had been the second torch-bearer the time before. He seemed to know his

54

way round the shrubbery rather well for a non-resident consultant. I shivered. Not because I was cold, but because my arm tingled where he had touched me.

He noticed it. 'Cold?'

'No,' I said. 'It wasn't a shiver. It was a—a *frisson*. If you know what I mean.' Then I felt stupid for saying it: the way he'd translate it wasn't the way I meant.

'Sorry if I startled you. I was looking for you, actually. Your chum Rose said you'd be on at ten, and I guessed you'd come this way.'

That 'Rose' really got under my skin. 'Look,' I said, 'Dr. Jones, you *can't* keep calling us by our Christian names. You're—you're a *consultant*. It just isn't on.'

He laughed out loud at that. 'If you'd ever worked in a psychiatric hospital you'd be less hidebound. Practically everyone is on first-name terms with everyone else. Nurses, doctors, and patients, certainly. It's only the gardeners who rate as Mister.'

I thought of Miss Carte. Her name was Helen, and it didn't suit her one bit. 'Not *Matron*,' I said, shocked.

'Well, perhaps not. But she'd call *you* by your first name. It makes a pleasant team spirit. And a nice sort of anonymity for the patients, too.'

I saw that point. 'You mean they can't go home and gossip about Mrs. Arbuthnot in the next bed, so to speak?'

'Sort of. There oughtn't to *be* any stigma—but a hell of a lot of people are still old-fashioned enough to think that mental illness is something to be ashamed of. Isn't it just as shameworthy to neglect your body until you get a gastric ulcer?'

'I suppose so,' I said. 'Only that was an unfortunate analogy—we've long ago accepted that gastric ulcers are a sign of nervous tensions anyway. If you'd said hepatitis from over-drinking it would have made more sense ... You're trying hard to indoctrinate me, aren't you? Why *did* you want to see me?'

'Because I've had a good idea about young Lynne. Or should I say Nurse Bache?'

We went on walking towards Iso while he talked, and I was aware of the glint of his eyes and teeth in the light from the frosted-glass window of the sluiceroom. 'What about her?'

'I may as well tell you that Sister Ross doesn't agree with me ... Seems to me it might be a good thing for both of them if we encouraged her to go sick-visiting with Tony Sugden now and again.'

We stood still outside the end door, where I could see him properly. He was studying me while I thought about it. Then I said: 'And what will Dr. Watterson have to say?'

'Does that matter?'

'Does it *matter*?' I let out all my breath at once. 'Dr. Jones, you're nothing but an anarchist! Look, I've had one hell of a bawling-out from Matron today for what she's pleased to call "disobedience". I'm sent on nights as a punishment, in case that fact had escaped you. I'm *not* going to take the responsibility of letting that girl run round visiting barrier-patients.'

'Oh, rubbish,' he said. 'A little healthy companionship between the sexes is a great panacea for a lot of things. I'm a believer in throwing young people together.'

I thought he was too cocksure altogether. 'The S.S.O. was dead right,' I said. 'He thinks psychiatry is a hundred per cent conjecture.'

That amused him. 'That's because I told him he was an obsessive ... Well, I'm supposed to go up to the gynae ward, to calm down somebody called Mrs. Baxter.'

'*Miss* Baxter,' I said involuntarily.

'Five children?'

'That's the one. Oh, you're going to deal with her low back pain?'

'I hope so.'

'Take my tip,' I said as he turned away. 'Get her out of Miss Fantague's orbit. *She* thinks everything's organic, too. She calls Iso the "faith-healing department".'

I could just distinguish the whiteness of his raised hand as he crossed the forbidden lawn to the main block.

Rose said: 'You do look funny. All ... No, don't tell me, let me guess. You met old Celtic Twilight in the grounds, yes?'

So I had not mistaken the S.S.O.'s dig after all. 'Right,' I said. 'Full of windy theories about getting Bache to frat with Tony for both their goods.'

Rose was settling her cap in front of the office mirror. 'He could be right, at that. He's not daft. What's all this about your being hauled off to Matron? Old Caudle didn't seem to have a clue why you'd come to nights.'

'Oh, it was Peters, really. She says Peters is irresponsible and needs supervision, so I had to swop with her.'

'Peters? I always thought she was quite a good nurse.'

'She is—but she did a stupid thing. Could have been any of us. If that Greene women wasn't such a confounded sneak——'

'Ah, now you're talking.' Rose turned round began to collect her bits and pieces, letter pad, library-book, bleeper, clip-board, and the rest of a night relief's paraphernalia. 'Now there's one I've not much use for. Ever seen her in Minor Ops? She takes about an hour to do one measly circum—Sister Connery goes up the wall about her. Oh, old Caudle says you're to take Peters's nights-off. Friday and Saturday, to begin with.'

'Fine,' I said. 'Couldn't have fitted in better. Can I move into Guerdon Road on Friday? Matron says snap. With the usual proviso about double beds and so forth.'

Rose said that would be great, and then looked up and down the corridor. 'I don't know where your junior's got to. She's a new one—Roberts by name—because little Hickin's got nights-off till Tuesday.'

I knew Roberts. She was said to have two speeds, dead slow, and stop. But she was willing enough. 'Right,' I said, 'I'll find her. Anything to report?'

'Nothing of any moment, that isn't in writing. Stanway's O.K. after her op. Tony's a bit restless, but he's had his sedative. Both the admissions have been sedated too. I hope you enjoy *them*.'

When she had gone I checked the admissions' details, and saw what she meant. One of them was a Mr. Fairbrother from E.N.T. One of Mr. Rimbaud's patients. He had come in originally for antrum puncture, but his headaches, previously diagnosed as sinusitis, were getting worse. The radiographer could find nothing wrong, and would Dr. Jones please see. The other was Alice Ratleigh, sent in under the S.M.O. for insomnia. According to the history she had had no more than a couple of hours' sleep for weeks. I wasn't very convinced. She had been given a couple of Mogadon tablets, I noticed. I hoped Rose had watched her swallow them. Not that it would have mattered if she had hoarded them by the dozen: people had been known to take as many as sixty with no more effect than a two-day sleep. That was the whole point of using them. I couldn't think why they didn't use them more often, instead of barbiturates.

At any rate, Ratleigh seemed to be sleeping when I did my round. If she wasn't she was a better actress than I took her for. And when I came to Tony Sugden's cubicle I saw that one of the barrier gowns was missing from the peg outside his door, and realised that I had at last found my missing junior. She stood beside the bed, looking at me helplessly. Tony, sound asleep, had a tight grip on her right hand. 'I didn't like to disturb him,' she explained. 'He said he'd go to sleep if I held his hand—and he did. I knew you'd be look-ing for me.'

'All right,' I said. 'He won't notice now—he's had a lot of sedative.' I curled his fingers back far enough for her to slip her hand away. He didn't stir. Outside, as we scrubbed, I made a sudden decision. 'Next time he wants his hand held, get Nurse Bache to go and do it. We're too busy. Dr. Jones seems to think she needs someone else to think about as well as herself. Only don't tell her so.' With Roberts one had to be explicit. 'Have you done all the four-hourlies? Yes? Then get on and clear up the sluice—it's a shambles —while I do the lists, and then we'll have some coffee. Any rounds done, apart from Dr. Jones?'

She was still drying her hands when I had finished. 'The S.S.O. came, Staff. He just checked on Nurse Stanway.'

'Right. I'll be with her if I'm not in the office.' I watched her fiddling with her hands. 'Do move, Roberts!'

Stanway was drowsy, but happy enough. 'I'm sorry I was such a fool,' she told me. 'But I've been worried so sick——'

'Who wouldn't be?' I said. 'Concentrate on getting some weight on. Like some Horlicks? It's supposed to put pounds on in nought seconds flat.'

'I'd love some. Can I?'

'Sure . . . and listen, Stanway. Nobody, except those who were involved, knows anything about your little experi-ment this morning. And they won't talk. All right?'

She looked relieved. 'So Sister Ross said—but I thought it'd be the topic of the week. Thanks.'

'Forget all about it,' I said. 'Lord, I do enough daft things myself when I'm scared.'

'*You?* And there was the S.S.O. telling me what a nice sensible girl you were, and how, but for you——'

'Little does he know,' I said. 'He's seen me in theatre, and scared to death of the Fantail, and thinks I'm a quiet little thing who never makes mistakes, I suppose. He should ask Matron.'

That was the wrong thing to say. Stanway frowned. 'You didn't get a rocket from her over—over me, did you?'

'Only a damp squib.'

'I suppose she'll be coming down to see me, too.'

'I doubt it,' I said. 'She'd be right out of her depth, and she knows it. She's all right on her own ground, sitting in that office like a spider, but I think the outer edges of the web make her nervous. I'll get your Horlick's. Anything else you want?'

There wasn't, she said. And then the phone rang softly on its night buzzer. Most people rang up to enquire between half past ten and eleven. When the pubs turned out, presumably. It was only natural that anxious relatives should go out and drown their sorrows for an hour or two, and then ring up and ask after their nearest and dearest on the way home. It was the same in all the wards, but in Casualty it was the peak time for accidents. Mums and Dads might be telephoning the hospital, but big brother would be out on his motorbike, and then *their* fond relatives would be ringing up.

Alice Ratleigh slept for a good six hours, claimed to have had her eyes open all night, and ate an enormous breakfast. It must have been nice to know that she'd successfully got away from geriatric. I didn't feel very charitable towards her, though I knew I ought to try, and I made up for my scepticism by taking her my own *Nursing Mirror* to read. Mr. Fairbrother looked like Tiny Tim, talked like Socrates, and only produced a headache when I was tactless enough to enquire after it—so that from six o'clock onwards he lay flat on his back with his legs contorted saying 'Oh, God!' at regular intervals. Tony grew restless towards dawn, and I had to give him the pethidine that was written up p.r.n.— which meant that he got it as and when he needed it, at the discretion of the nurse. I stretched my discretion a bit: I felt he deserved that.

The rest were fine, I told Caradoc when he came bursting in at eight o'clock. I added: 'I saw Dr. Jones last night. He seemed to think it would be a bright idea to encourage little Bache to hobnob with Tony. He said Sister didn't think much of it. What do you think?'

He ran his hand through his carroty hair a time or two and then nodded. 'Shucks, I don't know—but she's quite a little dish in her way. Might cheer him up. Why not, if he likes that sort of thing?'

'The idea was to do *her* good,' I pointed out. Take her mind off her own problems, as it were. But I must admit that I was thinking of it from Tony's point of view myself. That poor kid isn't going to have much chance to get among the girls. On the other hand, is it fair to whet his appetite?'

Caradoc said something vulgar about enjoying having his appetite whetted any time, and added that if Bache showed any signs of getting broody he would have another go at Sister about it.

'You do that,' I said. 'Can I go now?'

Caradoc stuck out his chest importantly. 'I don't know about that ... Now that I'm senior Staff on this ward——'

'You know what you can do with it,' I told him rudely. 'Goodbye. Have fun.'

All through night nurses' dinner—which proved to be a non-early-morningish Irish stew, with Bakewell tart and custard to follow—I was thinking about moving to Guerdon Road. Rose had given me a key during the night, when we met at Meal, and it looked like a good idea to get the first instalment of my gear up there straight away, instead of waiting till next day. So before I went to bed I rang Geoff.

'Oh *no!*' he said, when I told him I'd gone over to nights. 'Not again! It's only three months since you were on in Casualty—and I could nip in and see you there.'

'Well, you can't nip in and see me in Iso, I assure you,' I told him. 'People have been shot at dawn for less. Anyway, what I wanted to ask you was whether you could drive up this evening, early, and help me take some of my stuff to the flat. I'll be moving in there to sleep tomorrow, but I thought I'd take my trunk and things up today. If you came straight from the site I could be ready by about a quarter to six—and then I'd get back in time for night breakfast.'

'Could do,' he said reluctantly. 'And if you've got anything unwieldy it'd *better* go today, because I won't be able to help you tomorrow. I've got a—a business dinner to go to.'

'There, and me with a night off,' I said. 'Still, I'll be off on Saturday as well, so——'

It would have been normal if he'd then said that he'd pick me up on Saturday afternoon. But he didn't. He only said, in a vague kind of way: 'Oh? Well, we'll have to see . . .'

'But you'll come tonight?' I pressed.

'Oh, sure. Yes. Be there by a quarter to six. That's at the Home?'

'At the Home, yes.' Where did he expect to pick me up? I wondered impatiently. From the mortuary?

He certainly didn't arrive at the Home at a quarter to six. Or at a quarter past, either. And when I rang his home number the line was repeatedly engaged, and the site wasn't answering. By half past six I sat fuming on my trunk in the front hall realising that unless he turned up stat. I wouldn't have time to get back and change in time for seven-thirty breakfast. Not that I cared if I missed the meal, but I cared very much that old Caudle should not, so soon after the Stanway incident, have any reason to report me to the office.

At twenty-five to seven, when time was running right out, the Home porter came through, put his hands on his hips, and said: 'Gone and forgotten you, has he? Where was it you got to go?'

'Guerdon Road,' I said. 'But I've about had it now.'

'*Guerdon* Road? Hold your horses, Staff. I think I can fix you. One of our men's just off up there. Hold on.'

I had always thought that Ben had sense, that he had been at Teddy's long enough to know how many swabs made five. So I only felt pleased when I saw him go to the phone and dial his oppo at the car-park gate. Anything that Ben fixed would be sure to be just the job.

I went on thinking that until he came back. Then he said, 'Be round here for you right away, Staff.'

'What is it, an ambulance?' That, or the blood bank van, was the most likely. It wouldn't be the first time I'd scrounged lifts from either.

'You're joking,' he said. 'A Volvo, isn't it?'

'A *Volvo*?' Only one of our men—and he was a consultant—used a Volvo. I wanted to die. 'Ben, how *could* you! You haven't asked Dr. Ffestin-Jones for a lift? A consultant? Oh, really!'

Ben only grinned. 'If he don't mind, I don't see what call you've got to kick up,' he said amiably. 'He's a good bloke. Do anything for anybody. Knew him when he was on the house, before he went off to the Maudsley to learn the trick-cycling stuff.'

I wasn't going to be able to get out of this one. The red and black Volvo was pulling in at the bottom of the steps.

CHAPTER FIVE

I RAN down the steps before he could get out of the car. 'Dr. Jones,' I said, 'this is a mistake. I'd no idea who Ben was talking about! I thought there was an ambulance or a sitting car or something that was——'

'So?' He got out and came round on to the pavement. 'The stuff'll go into this, won't it?'

'That isn't the *point*. He'd no business to ask you.'

'But I'm very glad he did. I live in Guerdon Road—the least I can do is to help a new neighbour. Why do you want to be so anti-social?' He put me gently to one side. 'Hold on, Ben. I'll give you a hand with that.'

New neighbour was good. It wasn't surprising that he lived in Guerdon Road: a lot of consultants did—at the other end, where it was all Regency stucco and wrought iron. Even in the middle there were beautiful old houses where a couple of dozen surgeons and physicians had their rooms, or kept town flats. But number 53, where Rose lived, was a Victorian Gothic villa with added bay windows, and curlicues on the barge-boards of the gables, and had every variety of curtain proclaiming its multi-occupation. We should hardly be neighbours. I only hoped that Lydia Pike was not in her office to see him manhandling my trunk with Ben. I ran back for my two holdalls while they did that, and scribbled a message for Geoff on Ben's telephone pad, and then Dr. Jones was there in the hall again asking: 'Right? That the lot?' I was never so embarrassed in my life.

'Just these I'm carrying,' I said. 'But I feel terrible about this.'

'Then don't.' He smiled at me. 'You're wasting nervous energy. Are you on duty tonight?'

'Yes. I've got to be back by half past seven, for night

breakfast.' I got into the passenger seat and closed the door before he could reach it, and waited while he started the engine. 'You see, Geoff——'

'He of the watch?'

'Yes. He promised he'd be here at a quarter to six, and he wasn't, and I can't contact him, or——'

'Good,' he said. 'When you do track him down you can thank him for giving me the pleasure. What number Guerdon Road?'

'Not the grand end, I'm afraid. Fifty-three.'

'That'll be near the park entrance? Quite nice. I'm not at the grand end myself, either. I run a flat around the middle thirties. I share rooms there, too—with Rimbaud and a couple of Queen's men.'

I knew Mr. Rimbaud's rooms. I had taken a private patient there a few times. 'Number thirty-three,' I said. 'I know it. It's a lovely house. A pity it had to be divided up. But at least there aren't any horrid nameplates to spoil the frontage ... That's why I didn't know you were there too.'

'But I wasn't, until this year. I had a rather nasty little room in an office building, in Monument Lane. And then Rimbaud got married and left the flat, and at the same time a fellow from the Eye Hospital retired and gave up his rooms, so there I was.'

He swung left off the Hagley Road, and I waited until he had changed up again, and asked: 'Where did you live before?'

'Where I officially do now—in Four Oaks. But the flat's handier, and I'm here more than I'm there. And you?'

I suppose I would somehow have managed to tell him without reacting too much that my home was at Shenstone Woodend, just three miles further than his. Only I didn't get the chance. His arm flashed across my chest like a whip as both his feet went hard down together. 'Damned idiot!' he said. The motor-cyclist who had cut in on him was fifty yards away before I could fill my lungs again. Then he turned to look at me. 'I'm sorry about that. Didn't crack your sternum, did I?'

'Not quite,' I said. 'It was the shock.'

'Sorry. I do it instinctively if I have to brake hard. It's—it's a habit.'

When we turned into Guerdon Road I had enough breath to compliment him. 'It was the quickest thing I ever saw in my life. Your reactions must be frightfully fast.'

'They should be,' he said briefly. 'I'd probably have done it even if you *had* fastened your safety-belt. Why didn't you?'

I looked at his, lying loose. 'Why didn't *you*?'

'It's too long a story, at this moment ... Ah, there's number fifty-three.'

I helped him to lug my trunk and cases out on to the porch and looked up to thank him. 'It's very good of you. I *am* grateful. I hope it hasn't made you late for anything.'

'I haven't finished yet.' He looked down at the trunk. 'Which floor?'

'Oh, first,' I said. 'But I'll get someone to give me a hand. There's no need for——'

While I was talking, he was heaving it on to his back. I gathered the rest and followed him. On the landing he said: 'O.K., you go ahead and open the door.' And when he had finally dumped it in the second bedroom: 'What the hell do you *have* in there? Bodies?'

'Sorry. It's the books and the shoes that make it heavy.'

'And you thought you and your friend Rose could carry it?'

'Rose has already gone,' I said. 'She's not in her room, at any rate. Look, I'd make you coffee or something, but I've no time. I'll have to run.' —

'Run be bothered.' He took my elbow and steered me down the stairs again. 'I'll take you back. And don't argue. It won't take five minutes, and I've nothing more urgent to do.'

Half-way along Monument Lane we caught up with Rose, plodding along on foot, and he picked her up too. She said: 'How nice. I've always wanted to ride in a Volvo. What year is it? My uncle has the one before this.' And from then on she did all the conversing. I never knew she was so mechanically minded.

I said as much when she sat on my bed while I changed. 'Where d'you get all this car talk? Stealing the thunder!'

'Oh, how to get your man. Lesson One: swot up car jargon. Lesson Two: understand golf, soccer, rugger, and fly-fishing. Lesson Three: know what the *Financial Times* is all about.'

'And you do?'

'Well, I try. The way to a man's heart isn't through his stomach any more. It's through his twin carburettors or his new putter, old dear. You're not with it.'

I dragged on my clean apron, and picked up my blue belt. 'If it means all that swotting I'd rather be without it, thanks.' I looked at her in the mirror as I settled my buckle. 'Does it take all that to keep Peter Ellis on his toes?'

She looked surprised. 'Actually, Peter Ellis is a dirty word, right this minute.'

'Oh?' I turned round to look at her properly. 'That's new, isn't it?'

'Fairly. Anyhow, there isn't time to yatter about it now. Come *on*, or we'll have old Caudle on our backs.'

That was as far as we went.

It was half past nine when Geoff rang through to Iso. It had been a waste of time to ask him not to ring me on duty: he always did exactly as he liked, and I was irritated when I heard his voice. 'Geoff,' I protested, 'I've *told* you——'

'I know you have. So what? Don't be so unreasonable, Didi. I had to ring up to explain why I couldn't shift your luggage. Couldn't get in touch before.'

'Hurry up, then,' I said impatiently. 'Go on, explain.'

'It was this house. The one I wanted you to see.'

'Well?'

'Well, I've bought it. Or rather, Dad's bought it for us. We had to jump in quickly—there wasn't time to get you, and anyway you'd have said you couldn't come. It was such a bargain—I can't tell you about it on the phone—but we had to say "snap" today or not at all.'

I didn't know what to say. 'It's not modern, is it?'

'No. It's just the sort of thing you usually like.'

'And when do *I* see it?'

'Next week some time? I'll fix it. Tomorrow I'm booked up, and——'

That was where I made a decision. 'And I'll be going home on Saturday. I haven't been for weeks.' I could see Miss Caudle coming across the grounds, hunched into her cape in the dusk. 'Have to go now. 'Bye, Geoff.' I put the receiver down just in time. 'I've not come to do me round, Staff Nairse,' old Caudle said. 'You can carry on. I just want the loan of yer tracheotomy set. Some curless pairson's left the Casualty set unsterile and I can't wait to boil it up, and you're the nearest.' The old girl was breathless.

I got the set from the sterilising-room. 'Shall I nip over with it, Sister? Give you time to get your breath back.'

'Perhaps yer junior——'

'She's in a barrier cubicle,' I pointed out. 'I'll go.'

I shot across to Cas and pushed the box at Miss Greene. She snatched it, and said: 'About time, too!' I felt like thumping her. Anyone else would at least have thanked me. And if her boss, Pete Hawkins, had been on duty he would have added: 'Bless you, Staff.'

I said all that to Sister Caudle when I got back, just to let off steam, but she shook her wise old head at me. 'Nay, you were put out when you came from the telephone, Staff Nairse, when I came in. It wasn't Miss Greene, it was you.' She patted my arm. 'You don't want to wairk yerself up. Take life as it comes. Yer'll never make a nairse if yer let things get on top of yer.' She waddled off then.

Roberts came out of Tony's room and blinked at me. 'Is Sister Caudle cross? I could hear her voice going. I thought maybe you were looking for me ... Tony says can Bache go and have her late drink with him: Sister Ross let her go in for tea, he says.'

'Oh yes. If *he* wants her.'

'He seems quite struck!'

'And what about her?'

Roberts smiled complacently. 'She's fine, Staff. No pains, no tantrums, nothing. So maybe Dr. Jones was right?'

'Maybe,' I agreed, 'but I don't want her in and out of there at all hours. Understand? Just twenty minutes to-night. I don't want that boy overtired. And I don't want him bored, either. I'll be with Mr. Fairbrother if you want me.'

Bache was in young Fairbrother's room when I got there. No, nobody had given her permission, she said, but they'd met in the corridor outside the bathroom and he'd invited her in. When I'd sent her packing I said: 'Now, Mr. Fairbrother, this isn't a holiday camp. You don't have other patients in your room without permission. Not female

67

patients, anyway.'

He lay on his back and looked at me lazily. 'She's a nice chick. Part of the therapy, I'd have thought. I'll have to have a word with Dr. Jones about her.'

'I don't care who you have a word with. She doesn't come in here unless *I* say so, when I'm in charge.'

He lifted his eyebrows. 'Dear, dear, we *are* in a paddy! What's happened to the image? The cool figure in white, as my friend Thurber had it? The tender loving care? The dedication?' He looked at my identity brooch as I leaned across him to reach down his chart-board. 'Staff Nurse D. D. Jones. Ah, that's it. Dedication Jones. *Devoted* Dedication Jones. That's what I shall call you.'

I told Roberts that bit, when we were having our coffee. 'Dedication Jones!' I fumed. 'I never felt less dedicated in my life than I do when I'm in his room. Why we should wait hand and foot on that one, who's nothing but an all-out lead-swinger——'

Roberts looked at me solemnly over her cup. 'Staff, you'll be sorry you said that, if he does turn out to be a glioma.'

'A *glioma*?' I stared at her. 'Where did you get that idea? The X-rays showed nil abnormal.'

'Well, I was here before you, and while I was waiting the S.S.O. was on the phone to Mr. Rimbaud in the office. And he said something about a glioma of the—the optic some-thing.'

'Optic thalamus?'

'That's it. And then he asked Nurse Peters if Mr. Fair-brother had complained much about his vision, and——'

'Yes, he does, when his headache is on.'

'That's what she said. And the S.S.O. said maybe the new X-rays would show something, and then he was talking about ventri—you know.'

'Ventriculography?'

'Yes. So perhaps he *doesn't* put it on.'

I sighed. 'Sorry, Roberts. I wasn't seriously suggesting that he did. Not consciously, I mean. I'm just in a bad mood, and I don't like him very much.'

She was an odd child. 'Sister Tutor told us that when we don't like a particular patient we must try to find some-thing in them to pity.' She reddened. 'Still, you know all that.'

'Yes. But thank you for reminding me, Roberts. If that *is* a glioma, then I sincerely pity him. Still, I don't imagine he realised the possibility.'

'Oh, he might. He's a terror for wanting to know all the whys and wherefores, and the S.S.O. is the sort who might explain to him, too ... I just never know what to say to people when they ask questions.'

'You do know what to say,' I told her. 'What did Tut tell you?'

She nodded. 'Yes, I know. You have to say: "I'm sorry, I can't discuss his condition. You must talk to Sister." Only that always worries them more, don't you see? They think you're hiding something awful.'

'It doesn't matter. Until you're State Registered you *can't* take the responsibility ... and when you are, it isn't always very pleasant, either. We can always pass the buck to the doctors, but it isn't easy for *them* to break bad news. But somebody has to do it.'

All the time I was talking I was thinking about Geoff, and the new house, and how I was going to break it to him that I wished he hadn't bought it, and that I still wanted to stay on at Teddy's. I knew there was no question of getting married and still working. He had made it plain enough at the outset that he had no intention of having a working wife. 'What would people think?' he'd said. 'They'd think I couldn't afford to keep you? It'd look so bad.'

I found Stanway awake and talkative just before Meal— she said she'd had so much sleep during the day that she wasn't sleepy—so I took her a cup of tea and sat down to talk to her about it for five minutes. And she said: 'Well, you know what our Freudian friend would say? He'd say you just didn't want to marry this chap, anyway.'

'That's silly,' I said. 'Of course I do. We've been engaged for ages.'

'That's not evidence. If it was, would Innes still be running around single?' She shook her bandaged head at me. 'Come off it. If you really wanted to marry him, you wouldn't let Teddy's stop you. You're not all that dedicated, surely?'

I got up. 'I don't know. I've already been called "Dedication Jones" once tonight. But I *don't* want to chuck up my job just when it's getting really interesting. Just when I've got some responsibility. Staffing's the best time. You can do it all, and you know it all, but you've still got a ward sister to pass the buck to if you get stuck. It's the year when you learn most, according to Matron. And even she can't be wrong all the time.'

I sent Roberts to First Meal. I wasn't hungry. And as soon as she had gone a complete stranger, in a registrar's white coat, walked into the office. I stood up. 'Good evening. I don't think I know you.'

'But I know *you*. You're Staff Nurse Jones. Correct? My name's Walsh. I'm Dr. Ffestin-Jones's clinical assistant. I don't strictly begin until Monday, but I'm just finding my way about.'

His handclasp was quick and hard, and went well with his square jaw. He looked like a rugger man, and he was wearing a Bart's tie. I said: 'You're from London?'

'There's an observant girl! That's what I like to see. Yes, I've been doing my D.P.M. at Bethlem and Maudsley. I'll be going back there, if I have my way. But I'm getting in a year's experience in the outer darkness of the provinces first.' He grinned. 'Go on, jump down my throat!'

I said I'd long ago learned not to rise to that sort of dig. 'What Birmingham does today, London does tomorrow,' I told him.

'Not in psychiatry, mate,' he assured me.

'That's because you breed more psychiatric cases in the city,' Dr. Jones told him from the door. 'Up here we're all so beautifully normal. Why are you wasting your talents on Staff Nurse Jones? *She* doesn't have any problems.'

That was what he thought. If he had been alone I might very well have cried on his shoulder and landed him with quite a few.

When they had gone, and Roberts was back, I went over to Meal myself. It was quite good, for once—fresh salmon, hot, with new potatoes—but I still wasn't hungry.

I had meant to sleep in the Home on Friday, but by morning I had decided that the sooner I transferred myself to Guerdon Road the better I would feel. I could easily carry the rest of my belongings if I left my cape in the changing-room. So I left my new address with the front office, and with Miss Pipe, and set off after dinner. Rose, who had been to the office, caught me up before I had gone far. 'Right,' she said, 'what shall we do tomorrow? I've just the one night off.'

'Come home with me?' I suggested. 'Be a change.'

'Love to. But aren't you going today?'

'Well, not until I've had some sleep. I'm dropping off now. I can't think why I'm so tired—it's absurd.'

She looked me over. 'Mental tiredness, maybe? You worrying about something?'

'Well . . . Geoff's bought a house. Or his father has. And I can't get myself excited about it. I know I ought to, but I just can't. It all seems to be closing in on me.'

'What, marriage? Or just marriage with Geoff?'

She was as suspicious as Stanway, I told her. Then I said, 'Actually, I'm just beginning to wonder whether you and Stanway are right. But I'd *know*, wouldn't I? I mean, if I'd gone off Geoff I wouldn't want him to—to kiss me and so on, would I? And I do.'

'Ah, that's just the tender trap, old dear. The demon Sex rearing its ugly head. There's more to marriage than shacking up with somebody, after all. I mean, one doesn't marry the seaside flirtation. When I think of some of the gorgeous men I've met, at dances and things . . . Wow! But I wouldn't think of *marrying* them. Maybe you really only wanted an affair.'

That was funny. 'Don't be absurd,' I said. 'Geoff isn't that sort. He couldn't dally if he tried.'

'Oh, I know what sort he is! He marries property. A house—preferably one much too grand for him—and a status-symbol of a car, and lots of expensive furniture. Adornments for his ego. And then, of course, he has to have a wife to go with them. Somebody to look after this house and furniture. Somebody to comfort him with apples and all the rest of it. Somebody to buy rocks for, to show how prosperous he is. If you marry him, dear girl, you'll just be a—a chattel.'

I had never heard her so vehement about anything. 'Rose, you're being ridiculous. Geoff isn't one bit like that.'

'Then what is he like? Go on, tell me.'

'He's very—he's very kind, for one thing.'

'And generous?'

'Of course. He wants me to have a decent house. Yes, of

course he's generous.'

'That why you go shares on your outings?'

'Well, no. That's just because he thinks it's the right thing to do, when you're engaged.'

'What *he* thinks. Exactly. Do you know, ever since you've been engaged to him it's been "Geoff thinks this" and "Geoff thinks that". I'm tired of hearing it. Don't *you* ever think?'

'Of course I do, but——'

'You're beginning to, maybe. Well, carry on with the good work ... Look, if you go home today, I could come by bus tomorrow, couldn't I? Will your folks mind?'

'Of course not. Anyhow, I've got a double bed, if they're full up.'

'Good God!' Rose said. She looked over her shoulder. 'Don't let Matron hear you say that! We shall be drummed out of the Brownies if it leaks out. You know, her mother must have been frightened by a double bed before she was born, or something.'

'Geoff thinks the double bed is the "bedrock of married life",' I said.

'Cheaper than two singles, that's why.'

I was beginning to wonder whether I knew Geoff at all, or whether it was a case of the spectator seeing more of the game.

I thought so again when I reached home in the early evening. Freda was in alone—Father, she said, was at his Lodge dinner, and Mother had gone to the Parish Council meeting. She was lying flat on her back in the sitting-room listening to Peter Sarstedt records, and she looked nearer sixteen than twenty-six. The first thing she said was: 'Oh, you haven't got old Stuffed-Shirt with you, have you? Good. He'd never approve of this micro-skirt and I can't be bothered to change it.'

'Geoff?' I said. 'Do you see him like that, too?'

'Too?' She leaned over to switch off *Where do you go to, my lovely* and sat up. 'Who else does?'

I sat down in Father's big chair and looked at her. 'Oh, I don't know. Nobody seems to approve of him any more, somehow. As a partner for me, I mean.'

'That's no change. *I* never *did*. Since you mention it, I've always thought he was a sight too dull and commercial for you, but I've never dared to say so. Not that it's my business—you can marry some squawking pop-singer for all I care—but as you're not wearing your ring I take it you're having second thoughts.'

I looked down, surprised. 'I must have forgotten it!'

'Ah, how revealing are the things we forget to do.' Freda stood up and ruffled my hair. 'I may be a plant biologist, ducky, but I do know a bit about psychopathology. We do the things we want to do, and we forget the things we don't want to do: it's as simple as that. Want some tea?'

We had just twenty minutes together before she went careering off with two young men in an E-type Jaguar. She said they were lecturers, but they behaved more like first-year students. Jack and Selwyn. They wanted me to go too, but it would have meant riding on the hood, or on someone's lap, and I wasn't in that kind of mood. Instead I had a long hot bath and went to bed early with a new Muriel Spark. Geoff didn't approve of Muriel Spark, I reflected. He had found Miss Brodie unsavoury. Maybe he was stuffy, and I hadn't realised it? I had never compared him with other men before. He had simply been Geoff, and that was that.

Rose arrived while Mother was out shopping, and I made some coffee right away and yelled to Freda to come down. She'd been pretty late coming in, I think, because she came yawning in, in a brief kimono, and said that coffee was just what the doctor ordered, and where did these medical types get their energy?

'Meaning us?' Rose said. 'We don't. It's just an act we put on. We're all dead inside. Stiff upper lip and all that.'

Freda yawned again. 'No, not meaning you. Meaning that gang from Queen's, actually. Jack and Selwyn dragged me off to their dance last night. What a madhouse!'

I said that maybe it was their last fling before they settled down and cultivated a bedside manner. 'Same like theologs,' I suggested. 'They're as mad as hatters until they get made into curates and things.'

'Oh, not the *students*, my dear. I grew out of them long ago. The pukka quacks. Barney somebody, and Peter somebody, and a fellow called Courtney. And a ghastly jolly-hockey-stick woman who talked about nothing but Great Ops I Have Done. What was her name? Anthea.'

It was too late to head her off. I knew that Barney Kelly and Courtney Welch were Peter's friends and co-registrars. Rose was already asking: 'Peter Ellis?'

'Ah yes, that was it. Rather a sweetie, I thought. Terribly good-looking. You know him?'

'Slightly,' Rose said, as though she merely knew him by sight and wasn't in the least committed. 'He used to be at Teddy's.'

Freda looked at me reproachfully. 'You never told *me* you had anything as dishy as that.'

'No,' I said. I got up to fetch more milk. 'For the very good reason that he's already fully occupied. So you can keep your predatory little claws away from him.'

When I came back she was telling Rose about the new job she'd landed for the autumn. 'Well, I'll be based on the plant breeding station, near Aberystwyth, of course. And I'll have to do a spot of lecturing at U.C.W., I suppose. But there'll be quite a lot of travel. They want me to go to Canada before Christmas, and Denmark in the spring.'

'To do what?' I asked.

'Oh, to compare notes on this new project for increasing productivity of grassland and such. Pick their brains, if I can. Giving them the impression, of course, that they're picking mine. Why the devil did I do that thesis on grass populations for my Ph.D.? I'd far rather be working on forestry. Still, I shall enjoy the globe-trotting. Look out, Canada, here I come!'

It was when I turned to refill Rose's cup that I realised something was wrong. I knew her rather nice face pretty well, and it was obvious to me that something had hit her, hard. But I said: 'Rose, you're asleep on your feet, old thing. Come on, upstairs with you. If you don't want to go to bed you can at least have what Mother calls a "nice lie-down".' I shooed her out of the room as fast as I decently could. Upstairs I said: 'What on earth *is* it?'

She sat on the bed, looking up at me. 'British Columbia,' she said. 'I'll bet you anything you like. Grass, farming—it all ties up.'

'So?' There was some message I wasn't receiving.

'So that's where Peter Ellis is going.'

74

'Since when?' I sat down too. 'You didn't tell me.'

'Tell you? *I* didn't know until this morning. He only made up his mind this morning. I knew he was in line for a job, but they gave him a week to make up his mind. He made it up last night ... Well? Can't you see? It all ties up.'

'You mean—with *Freda*?'

'Of course. Face it, she obviously took to him. And he'd be sure to fancy her—she's the long-legged type he always looks at. And he does make up his mind suddenly, just like that. That's why I've been edgy—because he was even considering it. I've been holding my thumbs and praying for him to turn it down. And now this happens.'

'You are imagining things,' I said. 'Get your head down, and I'll call you at lunch-time.'

Downstairs I asked Freda which part of Canada she would be in. 'Didn't I tell you?' she said. 'Oh, Vancouver, principally. And around the rest of B.C., I suppose. That's where they've started this project, anyhow. Nice climate. Why?'

I did just have the sense not to tell her about Peter. And I had no intention of telling Rose that she was right, either.

Father was late for lunch, and pretty moody while we were having it. He looked at me oddly once or twice, too. And then, when we were having coffee, he said: 'A good thing that young man of yours isn't working for Grafton and Chelwood.'

I looked up. 'Why? They're a good firm, aren't they?' I was puzzled. 'Your department gives them plenty of work.'

'Not any more, it won't. I had to go in for a special enquiry this morning. otherwise I'd have got on with those sweet pea sticks. There are two young civil engineers—not unlike your Geoff—resident engineers on the new by-pass road, who have been doing very nicely, thank you, out of Grafton and Chelwood.'

Freda chipped in: 'Taking hand-outs, you mean?'

'Rather more than hand-outs ... One of them had a three-week holiday in Spain paid for. The other has had fifty pounds a month put on the desk in the site-office, *and* was told to go and choose himself a ciné camera or a tape-recorder, or whatever he fancied, and charge it to them.

75

And now they're offering him a brand-new car.'

Mother looked shocked. 'Oh dear! And I suppose all that really comes out of ratepayers' money, does it, Gerald?'

'Not only that, but the ratepayers aren't getting the quality of job they're paying for.'

Rose and I, simultaneously, asked: 'How did you find out?'

'The way these things usually do get out.' He looked apologetically at Mother. 'Because women talk. And the first chap's wife talked, and the other's fiancée. Showing off, d'you see. Well, they won't have the opportunity to talk again. Not so far as the City Council's contracts are concerned, at any rate.'

'I'm sure that Bright, Richards, and Lockyer wouldn't do that sort of thing,' I said loyally. 'Geoff's father would never——'

Father looked sardonic. 'Geoff's father is no better than any other contractor. Nobody gets a lot of big contracts without skating on thin ice. But some of them are too clever to fall through it. Look, I did the quantity surveying on those flats behind your hospital, didn't I? And I can tell you *they* definitely didn't go up without a few queries on specifications. B.R. and L. are up to all the tricks in the book, Didi. They're in business to make the till-bell ring, not to beautify the landscape.'

'That's right. They're in business to buy you a house, and things like that,' Freda said. She clapped her hand over her mouth. 'Oh lord! I forgot.'

'What?'

'While you were in the garden getting those flowers for Rose's room, I answered the extension upstairs. Geoff rang. He said he'd come over this afternoon and take you to see it. Sorry.'

'Today?' I wasn't pleased. 'But he said Monday. And I've got Rose here, and——'

'We'll look after Rose,' Mother said. 'You won't be more than an hour or so, will you?'

Freda nodded. 'No, you won't. He said he was just taking a quick flip out here and back, and that he had to be home again by six. People coming for drinks, or something.'

'Do you mind, Rose?'

'Good heavens, no, of course not. I'm going to help your

76

father in the garden.' She looked at him. 'May I?'

He said that he had been wondering how to persuade her.

In view of his lunch-time conversation it was hardly the day to expect him to welcome a contractor's son with open arms. So when Geoff arrived I was standing at the window with my coat on, and went straight out to the car. I was mentally comparing it with the Volvo, and he must—for once—have picked up my thoughts, because he announced: 'I'm going to ditch this crate soon. Got my eye on a G.T. model.'

'A pity you don't work for the Corporation,' I said. 'You might have got one for nothing. I hear that's the way these things are done nowadays.'

He didn't turn a hair. He didn't even trouble to deny it. 'Well, there are wheels within wheels, the same as in any other business, naturally.'

'You mean to say that B.R. and L., are paying out handouts? Bribes?'

'I wouldn't call it that. It's not as though any money changed hands. But if a fellow obliges us, we help him if we can. No use being mealy-mouthed about it. Never get anywhere that way.' He smiled at himself in the mirror. 'Never get any contracts that way.'

I felt cold. 'Why not?'

'Do you understand how local authority contracts *are* got?' His voice told me that I was being obtuse.

'Not really. I suppose you put in estimates, tenders, whatever they're called.'

'Precisely! And whatever they may say about not necessarily accepting the lowest tender, in practice they nearly always do. Right? So you've got to put in the lowest figure you possibly can. The lowest that'll give you a profit.'

'Yes, I see that. But I don't——'

'Look, suppose we're asked to tender for some road works. Let's say, for the sake of simplicity, that the specifications say we've got to use a ton of tarmac or what-have-you for every thirty square yards. All right, the total price *we'll* put in will really only cover the cost of three-quarters of a ton, because we underestimate on the labour. So it's a low price, and then we get the contract.'

'Yes.'

77

'Well then, when their resident engineer comes to check the levels and so forth, he'll do a bit of wangling with his blueprints and his figures, so that we only *need* to use three-quarters of a ton—or even less, if he's bright. So we can do it to a profitable price, and we can still afford to give him a cut—because without his help we'd never have got the contract.'

'So in fact you've got to fix it with him, to do that, before you even tender?'

'Of course. It's common sense.'

'Is that what you call it? I call it sharp practice,' I told him. 'I mean, it's the ratepayers' money.'

He slammed the gear lever across irritably. 'Look, Didi, if we didn't play along with the City chaps, where do you think you'd be now?'

'Right where I am, I suppose. What on earth difference does it make to me? *I* don't pay rates.'

He circled two more roundabouts before he said any more. Then he told me: 'You wouldn't be going to look at this particular house, for a start, if Dad didn't keep McKechnie sweet.'

'Why on earth not?'

He sighed. 'Oh lord, have I got to spell it out to you? Because they were going to build part of the ring-road through a certain block of houses. The city was going to pay a good price to get them and demolish them. So McKechnie nipped in and bought them very cheaply, before the plans were made public. Well, now the plans have been altered, because of the golf club kicking up about their precious course, so they're not going to make the compulsory purchase after all. Right? So McKechnie wants to unload them again—and we've bought one from him, much cheaper than it otherwise would be, and he still makes a profit, so we're all happy.'

I wasn't. 'But surely Mr. McKechnie isn't supposed to make use of inside information to——'

'Of course he's not "supposed" to! But if we all did what we were supposed to do none of us would ever get anywhere.'

I couldn't even trust myself to speak until I saw that we were on the Hagley Road. Then I sat up. 'Geoff, just where are these houses?'

'Pilkington Road, most of them. And a couple round the corner in Guerdon Road—your road.' He felt that I was surprised. 'Thought I'd told you.'

'No, you didn't.'

'There's only one that you'll like. The others are too rambling.'

I think I knew it then. It was the second from the corner of Pilkington Road. It was the smallest of that block. It was a lovely little Georgian house with a portico smothered in wistaria, and beautiful wrought-iron gates to the semicircular gravel drive. It was me—and I didn't want it. 'What number is it, Geoff?'

'Thirty-three,' he said. 'Why? The number doesn't matter. We'll give it a name. Wistaria Lodge would be nice—it's got the stuff growing up the front.'

I was right.

'Stop the car here,' I said. 'Please, Geoff.'

'What, right here?'

'Right here,' I said. 'Now.'

CHAPTER SIX

GEOFF pulled in to the kerb in Pilkington Road. 'Now what?' he wanted to know. 'I haven't got all day, you know. I'll have to be home sixish—we've got——'

'I know. "People for drinks." Mr. McKechnie, I suppose, and all the rest of the Surveyor's Department.'

He didn't know how to take that. 'The McKechnies, yes.'

'Plural?'

'Well ... His wife, and Isobel.'

I had seen photographs of Isobel McKechnie, in the *Post* and in the *Warwickshire Magazine*. She was the dumb-and-dewy type, straight from a Vevey finishing school. Very pretty, in a wondering kind of way. 'Oh, don't keep *Isobel* waiting!' I said. I meant it to sound sweetly mocking, but it didn't come out that way. 'In fact, you needn't waste any time showing me number thirty-three. I already know it. It's Mr. Rimbaud's house.'

'Some quack uses it, yes. He's only a tenant.'

'Yes, but you can't just throw him out. And there are three other consultants there, too. One of them lives in the flat at the top, since Mr. Rimbaud got married.'

'*Does* he?' Geoff looked as though all his Premium Bonds had come up at once. 'I see. Well, that simplifies matters considerably,'

'Why? You can't turn them out?'

'Indeed we can. Rimbaud's lease specifically precludes subletting except——'

'But he's done it for years!'

'Let me finish! Except for *non*-resident use as consulting-rooms. I understood he lived in the flat himself. But now you tell me it's sublet to somebody else. Right. That's a clear breach of contract, so he forfeits his lease. We can have the lot of them out in no time.'

I wished I could bite my tongue out. 'But you're not to, Geoff. Not on my account, anyhow.'

'You mean you don't like the house?'

Not like it? I loved it. It was more than I had ever dreamed of. The kind of thing I'd have given my ears for in other circumstances. I tried to explain this. 'It's probably the most attractive house, in our sort of size-range, that I've ever seen. All that lovely white panelling ... Of course I like it! Who on earth wouldn't? But I don't want it on these terms.'

Geoff scowled. '*What* terms, for God's sake?'

'To begin with, I don't like the way it was bought. And secondly, I can't see four consultants—two of them from Teddy's—turned out of their rooms, when rooms are so scarce.' I didn't mention the flat, but it mattered almost more than the other things, I think.

'So you want me to tell Dad that you're chucking it in his face, is that it?'

'No, Geoff, it isn't like that. It's just that——'

'It's just that you've no intention of getting married at all, isn't it?' Geoff had been flushed, but now he was white. That told me just how angry he was. Not upset; angry. 'Well? Go on, admit it. I'm just about tired of all this shillyshallying lately. I don't understand what's got into you.' And then, because I didn't answer, he went just too far. 'In fact, I'm seriously beginning to wonder whether *I* want to, that's the truth.'

'All right,' I said heavily. 'We'll call it a day.' I scrabbled uselessly at my empty third finger before I remembered. 'I'll give you your ring back, and we'll both think it over. Is that fair?'

'I don't *want* my ring back.' His lower lip came out sulkily, like a small boy's. 'Didi, there's no need to be so blasted dramatic about everything. All right, you don't like this house, so——'

'I didn't say that!'

'Well, you don't want to live in it. You don't want your darling doctors turned out. So ... There are plenty more houses to be had.'

I took a deep breath, and tried again. 'I'm sorry, Geoff. I'm right off even thinking about houses, at the moment. Or getting married. I want to stay at Teddy's for a while—I told you. And I want to feel free.' I began to open the door. 'I'll go back by bus. We can't have Isobel McKechnie put out, can we?'

'Don't be stupid!' He dragged me back by my arm. 'I'll drive you back.'

I let him. It was a whole lot easier. But we didn't do any more talking until we got to Shenstone Woodend. Then he said: 'Goodbye, Didi. I only hope you know what you're doing.' He seemed quite convinced that I was ruining my life for good. In a different mood I'd have thought that hilarious—the assumption that any girl in her senses would see marriage to him as the ultimate in achievement, and that only a complete fool would turn down the opportunity. At the time it merely made me feel a heel.

I told Rose all about it when I got her to myself. She must have given the family some sort of rundown, because nobody mentioned Geoff, or the house, or even threw me any knowing glances. Mother was quieter than usual, and Father was gayer, that was all. Freda didn't register anything.

Father drove us back to Guerdon Road on Sunday afternoon, so that we could put our feet up, as he called it, before we went on duty. I saw Rose scrutinising number 33 as we passed, but she didn't say anything and neither did I. I did notice that the wistaria was in leaf, and would soon be in bud. And when we were walking down to Teddy's I asked her—largely to keep her mind off Peter Ellis— whether she'd yet met Dr. Walsh. 'I rather liked him,' I said. I meant that she would, that he was just her sort, but it wouldn't have been politic to say so.

She nodded, 'Well, I haven't *met* him. But I did see something like that striding around. We exchanged the usual courtesies in passing, so to speak. What does it mean, exactly, "clinical assistant"? Does he rank as a registrar?'

'I suppose so,' I said. 'He's done his D.P.M., anyway. He's a Bart's man originally.'

'Yes, dear, I noticed *that*.' Rose was a tie-expert: what little knowledge I had was all gleaned from her. She knew on sight every university, every public school, every regiment, and every faculty of our local university. To say nothing of stray cricket and football clubs. Even glider clubs, the Press, and Oswestry Saints hockey team. She had a collection of ties hanging from the picture rail of her bedroom—battle trophies, she called them. One had bloodstains on it, from the time when Dennis O'Dea turned his Spitfire over and knocked out most of his front teeth. It was just before he married his physio girl, so maybe it was a stress accident. 'He also,' she was saying, 'has two fingers of his left hand amputated by half.' I hadn't noticed that, but Rose never missed anything. 'Probably why he took to psychiatry,' she theorised. 'Because he *looks* like a surgeon, really.'

I agreed. 'Yes, an orthopod type. Brawny.'

'Well, they have to be. Just look at some of the reductions they have to do. Takes a strong man ... Didi, *is* it all off between you and Geoff? Definitely, I mean? Just in case anyone should ask.'

'Who's likely to?' I frowned, trying to clear my mind. 'I just don't *know*, Rose. At the moment, yes, it's definitely and positively off. I feel really free tonight. It's a good feeling. I don't think I want to put my head back into the noose. The only thing is ... Well, have I been unfair?'

'You must be joking!' We stood still for a moment outside the door of the chatter-noisy dining-room. 'You wouldn't know how. *I'm* the unfair, love 'em and leave 'em, type. Not you. You're a confounded old stick-in-the-mud, if you want to know. Time you did show fight, if you ask me. Do you good to have half a dozen affairs in swift succession, my girl. That'd teach you to sort out the men from the boys.'

From someone who was about to lose her own steady, that was rather brave, I thought.

I found my Miss Baxter occupying one of Dr. Jones's beds that night. She was glad, she said, to get away from that Miss Fantague, and she reckoned that Dr. Whatsit-Jones was the cat's pyjamas. 'Trick cyclist, is he?' she asked.

'Psychiatrist, yes,' I told her distinctly. 'And a very good one. If he can't help you I don't know who can. Has he been to see you today?'

'Sat here twenty minutes or more. That Miss Fantague, she never gave me five minutes of *her* time. Mr. Gilpin, now, he used to chat me up sometimes. But he didn't cure my backache, did he? This Whatsit-Jones——'

'Ffestin-Jones.'

'Yes, well, this Dr. Jones ... He asked me all *sorts* of questions. You wouldn't believe! All about the fellers, and why didn't I marry 'em, and whether the kids were in care, and that. I told him I didn't want to tie myself down to anybody. Stands to sense. Married and done for, they say. No, me, I like my freedom.'

That made two of us. 'But is it freedom, when you've five children to think about?'

'Oh, I only ever have the youngest with me. The Children's Officer gets the others fostered, see. I like to have *one* about the place. I like kids. I could eat 'em.'

It seemed to me that it was possibly a pity that she didn't, in the circumstances. But it wasn't my job to say so. Not that Sister or I wouldn't give her a confidential chat, before she left, about limiting her output. Miss Fantague probably already had, but repetition would do no harm. The message might sink in, given time.

The S.S.O. came down early on, and he shut himself in with Mr. Fairbrother for a long time. When he emerged, about ten o'clock, he said: 'Let's both have some coffee, Staff. I want to talk to you.'

I told Roberts to finish the medicines for me, and take Stanway a pot of tea, and then I brought in two cups of coffee with the only staff saucer for him, and sat opposite him at the desk. 'There,' I said. 'Now I'm listening, Mr. Verrier.'

He got up and closed the office door. 'Oh, I know that's not done,' he said. 'But Matron's in bed, and I'm not afraid of Miss Caudle, and this is pretty confidential.' He settled himself in the swing chair and drank some of his coffee. 'About young Fairbrother,' he said at last. 'I've just had the fresh radiologist's report.'

I looked up sharply, remembering what Roberts had said. 'It's a glioma?'

'Yes. A pretty ungettable one, I'm afraid. Infiltrated into the hypothalamus ... It just didn't show on the other pictures. Considering its position, he's showing remarkably few signs. Headaches, a bit of ataxia, and Sister says he's not always rational.'

'No? I found him rational enough. A bit uninhibited, but he's that type. Cheeky, you know ... He calls me Dedication Jones.'

'And that's rational enough.'

'You don't know me,' I said. 'But he had little Bache in his room. Invited her in. He said she was "a nice chick". He doesn't think much of authority.'

'That all indicates a complete personality change, Staff. I know that boy. He's been in a couple of times—a semilunar cartilage, and an acute appendix—and he's always been excessively shy. He's a bit of a solitary, and he spends most of his spare time playing the cathedral organ ... Well?'

'You've succeeded in surprising me,' I confessed. 'I *have* misjudged him.'

'So, I rather think, did Mr. Rimbaud.'

I wondered whether a neuro-surgeon had seen him yet.

'No. Mr. Hutton has seen the pictures. He's examining him tomorrow. At the moment he's inclined to say——' He turned down the long thumb of his right hand.

'Oh no!'

The S.S.O. lifted both his arms and dropped them helplessly. 'It's very, very dicey. I just wanted to put you in the picture. Sister wasn't on when the report came through, and your Mr. Hughes doesn't know, either.'

'What have you told *him*? That's the thing.' I was thinking of what young Roberts had said about the S.S.O. being the kind to explain things. 'Does *he* know?'

He rubbed his jaw reflectively, a little guiltily. 'I went in there with the express intention of telling him a little about it. But somehow ...'

'You didn't get around to it?'

He shook his head. 'I did tell him that we weren't very happy about his X-rays. And I said Mr. Hutton would be seeing him. I got that far.'

'How did he react?'

'He gave it as his considered opinion that none of us knows his job, but that as long as he was having a nice rest he couldn't care less ... He said the stuff we were giving him wasn't enough to control the headaches—and that doesn't surprise me—so I've written him up for a quarter of morph., S.S.S.'

That reminded me. 'Oh, have you written up pethidine for Miss Baxter? I gather her papers aren't here yet, for some reason best known to Miss Fantague.'

'Or Andy Gilpin.' He smiled and pulled out his pen, and I passed him a fresh case-sheet of Dr. Jones's from the rack. 'Has Dr. Jones seen her yet, d'you know?'

'For a good twenty minutes, she says. She thought that was luxury, after Ward Five's quickfire methods.'

'Yes, she would.' He scribbled out the prescription and shoved the sheet over to me for completion. I filled the name in right away, before someone else got the pethidine by mistake. I had had enough drug problems for one week. 'But there,' the S.S.O. was saying, 'Dr. Jones has a lot more time than we have.'

'He needs it! People don't bare their souls in five minutes flat, S.S.O.'

He pushed his pen back into his white coat pocket and stood up. 'Miss Baxter hasn't *got* a soul, Staff.'

'She has! She likes babies. She says she could eat 'em.'

He said that I was telling him, and then he took himself off. I didn't see anyone but Roberts for the next hour, and then Dr. Walsh came down, with Sister Caudle puffing behind his long strides like a little shunting engine. They did a quick round, and then Casualty rang for her, and he lingered reading notes, and then looked at the empty cups and asked: 'Any left?'

'I'll make some. Tea or coffee?'

'Tea, please. No sugar. Fairly strong. In a large, thin cup, if possible.' He certainly knew what he wanted.

When he was on his second cup—he had Sister's own, it was the only thin one on the ward—he pushed the notes aside and noticed that I was still in attendance. 'Well, and how are *you*, Delia?'

'Who told you my name?'

'Ah, I have my channels. Mine's Rocky, by the way. Short for Rockingham, I hasten to say, and in no way connected with my bank balance. Delia, this is Rocky; Rocky, this is Delia. There, now it's all proper. So I'll repeat the query. How are you this evening?'

'Fair to moderate,' I said.

'That's not very good. *Why* only fair to moderate? I ask myself. Why the drooping *orbicularis oris*?'

'You mean the *risorius*,' I said. 'The *orbicularis* is for eating with. Think of *risus sardonicus* ... Oh, just personal things.'

'I salute your knowledge of anatomy. Mine stops short at the eyebrows these days ... The old love-life not going according to Cocker?'

'Psychiatrists!' I said. '*Everything* has to boil down to the love-life.'

'Usually does, sweetie. It's common knowledge that a depression in a young woman of under twenty-five is either a psychosis or it's reactive to the boy-friend situation. And I'm damn sure you're not psychotic.'

'I'm not depressed, either.'

'No? That too is a process of elimination. Your response to light chitchat is sluggish. *Ergo*, either you're depressed or you're allergic to one Walsh. And you're not allergic to Walsh, or you'd have left him to drink his tea all alone. Brought it in a thick cup too, as like as not. Well? Is that logic?'

Then I really did make a fool of myself.

Geoff would have said: 'Oh, for God's sake, don't *cry*!' and pretended not to be with me. Miss Fantague would have told me that this was a hospital, not a kindergarten. And Rose would have patted my back and waited for me to stop. Rocky Walsh only smiled approvingly, said: 'Atta-girl, let it rip!', and gave me three tissues from the box on the windowsill. Then he sat back in his chair and lit a cigarette.

He was lighting a second by the time I had blown my nose and pulled myself together. 'This one's for you,' he said. 'If anyone comes in, just shove it over my side of the ashtray. There won't be two going ... Now, feel like talking? You don't have to.'

'If I don't spill it to *some* neutral observer, I shall burst,' I said.

'And I'm no surgeon, so we can't have that. Spill away.'

He must have found it all pretty confusing, but he didn't say so. When I'd finished he said: 'Decisions don't upset people. Lack of 'em does. Your trouble is that you *haven't* decided. You want to have your cake and eat it too. You can't. Either you stay engaged, and recognise that this chap Geoff *does* have a right to marry you within the foreseeable future, or you break it off—*pow!*—like that and stop playing about with the idea. And confirm it in action. Live it. Go out with somebody else, just to ratify the decision.'

'*Who* else? Apart from my sister's crazy friends, and a few housemen who've stopped suggesting it, there's——'

'There's me,' he said mildly. 'Free, white, and twenty-nine. No strings.'

'*You?*' I stared at him blankly.

'Oh, girls do go out with me sometimes, I assure you! I don't think any of them have come to any harm, to date. What, Rocky, the pride of Bart's Nurses' Home, turned down? Never let it be said. Hell, I've been here three whole days, and you're the first girl I've asked out. I must be slipping. Well?'

'Some time, maybe,' I said. 'Thanks, all the same.'

'Make it soon. The passenger seat of my car is beginning to wonder what it's done. Since you don't ask—and they usually do, before they make up their minds—it's a Mini-Cooper S with a high-lift camshaft and——'

'Greek to me,' I said. 'Try that on my friend Rose.'

He was on his feet and ready to leave. 'Sounds very feminine.'

'She is,' I said. 'Staff Nurse Innes, to you. Night relief.'

'Dear me, I must investigate. What does she look like?'

'Fair, pink, pretty. Lively. A tonic *risorius*, usually.'

'And is *she* heartwhole?'

I shrugged. 'I think she's veering that way. She has her problems at the moment. Go and analyse her: I've got work to do.' I couldn't help noticing his left hand as he opened the door, and Rose had been right about his fingers. 'She thinks you look like a surgeon.'

He opened his eyes wide at that. 'So she has brains, as well as beauty, this Rose? How right she is.' He spread the damaged fingers in front of my nose. 'But for an unfortunate encounter with a size ten rugger boot I'd be a terrible swell called Mr. Rockingham-hyphen-Walsh by now. But actually, I'm glad I'm not. You can hack out just so many organs before the carpentry becomes a bore. Psychiatry's like midder—it's different every time. And there's always the odd miracle.'

After he had gone I checked again on David Fairbrother.

He was asleep, with half his blankets on the floor. He moved around, but didn't wake, when I tucked him up. I was glad of that: it meant I could hold off the morphia. He might have to be on it a long time. He looked about twelve in his sleep. I wished I had been nicer to him. Freda had always said that I was too quick to be prejudiced about long hair.

Alice Ratleigh put her light on when she saw me peeping through her porthole, and asked for tea and more sedative, so I purged my conscience by being nice to her instead. I took her a couple of Mogadons, and a whole pot of tea, and then I sent Roberts to First Meal and sat with her while she drank the first cup. I watched her swallow the tablets, too. Then I tried a leading question. 'They'll have replaced you on Geriatric by now, I suppose?'

'I should hope so. It takes two staff nurses to carry that half-baked Sister Toomes.' She looked at me sharply, and put her cup down. 'Does everyone think that that was the object of the exercise? To get away from Geriatric? Do they think I'm scrim-shanking? Well? Do they?'

'Of course not,' I said. 'But you couldn't blame them if they did. I mean, we all knew how you'd hate it. You're a darn good surgical nurse, and everyone knows it.'

'Well, you can tell them. Look, I didn't know I *was* going to Geriatric until last week, did I? And I've had insomnia for more than a month.'

'You've looked pale for a long time. Something on your mind?' It couldn't be love-life with her, I reflected. She didn't have one. She thought that men—apart from Sir Malcolm Sargent—were all half-wits. That meant all of them now.

'Everything. My father died three months ago. Now my mother's gone into Queen's with cervical carcinoma. She may do; she may not.'

'I'm sorry,' I murmured. 'No idea.'

'That's not the main worry. I've got an only brother. Ten. He's a mongol. If it doesn't work out, I'll be responsible for him. What can *I* do?'

'Who's looking after him now?'

'My grandmother. But that's useless as a permanent proposition. And I *won't* have him put in a residential place.'

'Did you tell Dr. Jones all this?'

'No. For a very good reason. I know exactly what would happen. He'd be pulling strings, and making arrangements, and before I knew it he'd have Dicky in some home before I could stop him.'

'He couldn't *do* that without consent!'

'Exactly. And my grandmother would consent like a shot. She's no patience with Dicky—and he's a sweet kid.'

'Yes, they're lovable little creatures ... Look, how long *could* she manage him? Or would you let him go into care just for a short time?'

'With what in view?'

'District training. Then you could have him with you.'

'But I'd need midder.'

'No. They're using a lot of general people on the district now, so that the midwives can stick to midder. In a lot of counties, anyway. Maybe not all.'

She looked at me for a long time, and then poured herself another cup of tea. Then she began to smile—I hadn't seen her anything but sour for ages. 'There's just one thing,' she said at last. 'Why the hell didn't *I* think of that?'

I went over to the door. 'Because you're just plain dim. Now get a good sleep.'

Rose was at Second Meal, and she looked a good deal more cheerful than she had at breakfast. She moved to sit next to me, and said, 'I've met this Walsh. His name's Rocky. He came trailing into Cas.'

'What on earth for?'

'Wanted some tea, he said. "In a thin cup, fairly strong, no sugar." He got it in Sister's thick Purbeck beaker, watered down, I'm afraid. Not that he grumbled.'

'Like him?'

'Great fun, I thought.' She dissected a lamb cutlet neatly and stacked the debris before she began to eat. 'I'm going out with him next nights-off.'

I might have known. Rose is always quicker off the mark than I am. 'Nice work,' I said. 'You'll be able to talk cars to him. He runs a hot Mini of some sort.'

'Yes, a Cooper S with a whole lot of mods. How did you know?'

'I don't know. Heard it somewhere.' If he hadn't told her about our conversation, I saw no reason to.

'He's going to let him drive it, too.'

'Good,' I said. 'Geoff never let me drive his Consul.'

'Consul!' Rose was contemptuous. 'I'm talking about a high-performance enthusiast's car, not a middle-class family saloon.'

'Oh well, he's swopping it soon. Getting a GT Cortina, or something.'

She sighed. 'And just what has that to do with you?'

Some chemical reaction must have taken place since I had unburdened myself to Rocky Walsh. Only I didn't know it until then, and it took me by surprise. I put down my spoon and blinked at Rose. 'Not a thing,' I said. 'Not a single thing. It's only just hit me. He can swop it for a tractor, for all I care. Or for one of his beloved J.C.B. earth-movers. Yes, he can go bumbling along in wasp-stripes at five miles an hour, with all the traffic hating him, and it doesn't affect *me* in the least. How right you are, Rose.'

'Then it *is* off?'

'Definitely, positively, absolutely.' I took a deep breath. 'Now I *know* it's the right thing to do. I feel marvellous. Great . . . Is there any more custard? I'm starving!'

The first thing I did, when I got back to the flat next morning, and had drunk the usual quantity of tea with Rose, was to pack up my engagement ring in its case and tissue paper, and go straight out to send it to Geoff by registered post. Never again would Mother be able to come up with little sayings about 'pearls for tears'. Never again would new housemen at hospital dances take one look at my left hand and sheer off. And never again would Freda call me 'Mrs. Lockyer' when she thought I was being squarer than usual. I felt beautifully irresponsible, and when I bumped into Andy Gilpin, with Jim Brabin, Mr. Davidson's H.S., rushing into the Grosvenor for a quick drink, I let them rush me in with them.

'But will they be open?' I said. 'It's barely half past ten. Surely they don't——'

Andy looked at me pityingly. 'When I save a barman's life—well, *he* thinks I did; actually it was a pure fluke—it makes me a fully paid-up, signed-in resident of any pub he happens to work in, chum. Officially the drinks are on him. Right?'

I didn't really care. 'We'll all go to jail together,' I said happily. 'That'll be nice. But only orange-juice for me, please, I'm frightfully thirsty. How you can drink horrid cold beer at this hour I shudder to think. Won't you be missed?'

He tapped his pocket. 'These new bleepers were specially rigged to reach as far as the Grosvenor. Save the porters racing up to get us.'

'As for being missed,' Jim said, 'Andy's got the Fantail's clinic.'

'Too right.' Andy leaned towards me. 'Staff Nurse Jones, Delia, Didi, have you ever taken that clinic? As for Jim, he's in the same boat with Pa Davidson.'

I knew what they meant. Gynae O.P. began at eleven-thirty, and there were still people waiting at five. And Mr. Davidson was getting slower all the time.

I left them talking to the barman, went back to the flat, had a hot bath and fell into bed. I didn't wake until Rose brought me some tea at a quarter to seven. She said 'Come on, Sleeping Beauty. I've had the television blasting away for more than half an hour, but you were dead to the world.'

I could still hear it. 'Anything interesting on the news?'

'Such as?' said Rose. 'No, not really. Oh, some stuff on the local news about corruption in high places, housing-wise. And people getting flooded out again at whatsit Avenue.'

'Charlecote Avenue?'

'I think so. A beefy type named Harris, leading the tenants on a protest march, all yelling like mad. I expect the cameramen put them up to it. They do, you know.'

I remembered Mr. Harris. 'That Harris is a nasty piece of work,' I said. 'A rabble-rouser.'

'I shouldn't think they *need* rousing! Not with all their carpets covered with mud, and their furniture wrecked before they've even paid for it. Be fair; they've got a case.' She finished brushing her hair, and turned round. 'Whose fault is it?'

I hated to think, after all Father and Geoff had told me.

'I've no idea.'

'Was the design wrong, or did somebody skimp the work?'

I was so used to being loyal to Geoff that I didn't even want to think about it. 'No idea. Did I tell you about Ratleigh and her problem? You may have suggestions.' I gave her the gist while I washed and dressed.

When she had thought it over she said 'Two thoughts. One, district. Two, why not get a job as a matron in a handicapped school, and have him with her? Nice little flat, telly, the lot, and not bad pay at all.'

I nodded. 'I always said you were bright.'

'Not bright, lovey, just plain crafty. With brothers like mine you learn to be . . . You ready?'

We had to run. It was one time when I'd have been very glad to see a cruising Volvo, but we had no such luck. We just managed to scrape into breakfast before Sister Caudle came to count heads.

Sister Ross looked at Nurse Roberts when we got to Iso. 'I don't think *you'll* be here long, Nurse , . . Make the most of her, Staff, before Miss Caudle fetches her away.'

Roberts turned bright red, and I said: 'Why, Sister?' I wondered what on earth Roberts could have done that I hadn't registered.

'Oh, nothing wrong! Sorry, Nurse Roberts. Did I frighten you? Well, you've had four patients discharged today—thanks to our superb nursing—so you can't expect a whole junior all to yourself, can you?'

'Four?' I twisted my head and tried to see the report.

'Four. The three sick nurses, and Tony Sugden. Tony was well enough to go back to his parents' care—they're very good with him, and his injections were finished. Nurse Bache has a week on sick leave, to see how she does at home. Stanway's G.P. can take her stitches out. And Ratleigh discharged herself and said she was going back to duty!'

I said: 'Do you know where, Sister?'

'I don't suppose she knows yet. Does it matter?'

'Not really, no. I don't think she'll be staying much longer, anyhow.' I reminded myself to get hold of Ratleigh and pass on Rose's special school idea. 'But I've still got

Fairbrother, haven't I?'

'Yes. No point in moving him back to E.N.T. Or in moving him anywhere until they decide what to do. Mr. Hutton's offered his parents the choice. It's fifty-fifty. He'll never do if they don't interfere, and he probably won't if they do. Not very cheerful.'

'When will they decide, Sister?' I glanced at Roberts: 'You mustn't discuss this, Nurse. You run along and see if you can get the laundry counted before I lose you, will you?'

'They'll be coming up tonight, I think. If they come to the ward, get the S.S.O. to see them, will you?' I didn't look forward to that interview very much. 'And you've got a couple of sick nurses. They're both first-years, both with 'flu, so I put them together for company. Rogers and Sinji. Easier for you—they'll have to be barrier-nursed, for Fairbrother's sake.'

'Quite.' I could see that she had more to say, even before she went over and closed the office door.

'There's just one more thing. After all the bad news about that young man, I do have one bit that's more cheerful.'

I studied her expression. Her eyes looked very bright. 'Personal, Sister?'

'You could call it that. But I expect it'll be public property by the time you've been to Meal. Oh, I've been a night nurse myself! Anyhow, you're the first to know ... It looks as if I'll be leaving pretty soon. In the autumn, anyhow.'

'You, Sister?' I stared at her. 'But last week you——'

'I know what I said. But it hadn't happened then.'

'I never did believe in that impacted tooth,' I said.

'What? But that was quite genuine ... Oh, I see what you mean. When I was out in the garden, talking. Yes, well, perhaps the company made me forget the soreness.'

'Dr. Jones?'

'Dr. Jones, Staff? You really can't be feeling well. Don't you want to know why I'm leaving?'

I dared to sit down on the corner of the desk. 'Could I guess, Sister?'

'Go ahead. What does the grapevine say?'

'It says that you and the S.S.O. are very well suited.'

She began to laugh. She was very pretty when she was

94

flushed. 'Then you can give it my compliments, and say that I think so too ... Oh, and you can see this. Take a good look, so that you give a full description.'

'This' was the most opulent-looking solitaire diamond ring I had ever seen, in shops or out of them. 'Wow!' I said. 'I do hope it's insured. What a *beauty*. I'd be scared to death of losing it.'

'You think I'm not? It's being made tighter tomorrow. Men, they never think of finding out your size, do they? But I wanted it just for one night.'

'Of course,' I said. 'You'll want to flash it round the sisters' sitting room. I do hope it all works out well, and that you won't miss Teddy's too much.'

'I won't. Not with my husband a consultant, bringing home all the gossip.'

'A—a consultant?'

'That's right. He's taking over from Mr. Davidson in September. He only heard today. Rushed out and bought the ring to celebrate.'

'Funny,' I said, 'I sent mine back this morning.'

Her face changed. 'Oh, I'm *so* sorry. If I'd known——'

'Don't be sorry, Sister. I'm not, honestly. It was all the most awful mistake. It would never have worked. Yours will.'

'You think so? I'm quite an old lady, you know. Thirty-nine ...'

'That's why,' I said. 'You won't make infantile mistakes.' I passed her cape over from the chair. 'Now I'll go and tell young Roberts. And *I'm* going to First Meal.'

Before I could even find Roberts the phone rang. The switch porter said: 'There was a Mr. Lockyer on the phone, Staff. I didn't put him through because I knew Sister hadn't come over yet. Wants you to ring him back.'

'Does he, George? Well, if he rings again will you tell him that I'm on duty, that I'm busy, and that we're not allowed to have personal calls on the ward. And that I'll ring him in the morning.'

'Just as you say, Staff. If you're sure. He sounded a bit put out.'

'I dare say he did. He usually is when he can't have his own way. You'd better remind him, if he rings, that this is a hospital, not a telephone exchange.'

'Very good, Staff.' I could almost hear the knowing grin on George's Sid James-type face. 'You *don't* want him put through?'

'I do not,' I assured him.

I didn't know how much I was going to regret that.

CHAPTER SEVEN

DAVID FAIRBROTHER's parents arrived long after I'd given up expecting them. His father was an aggressive little man, trying hard to camouflage the fact that he was scared silly by just being in a hospital ward; his mother was thin and gentle, and every now and then she would reach out and pat her husband's hand to calm him. He needed it. He talked incessantly while we waited for the S.S.O. 'What I want to know is, what did they *do* to the lad in that other ward? Never had a day's illness in his life before. What did they do to him? That's what I——'

'He had appendicitis,' I reminded him. 'And there was his leg. He got over those all right, didn't he?'

Mrs. Fairbrother nodded. 'That's right, Nurse, he did. Hush, Daddy! *They* wouldn't do him any harm.'

'Well, all I know is that he was a normal healthy boy until he came here. Now they're saying that he's seriously ill. It sounds very funny to *me*. What are we to think? Wash out his sinuses, the doctor said. Nothing in that. Next thing we know, they send him down here and they talk about operating on him. It isn't good enough. They just use people like him as guinea-pigs . . .'

I was glad when Mr. Verrier came. After a while he brought Mrs. Fairbrother out to me in the kitchen and said 'How about a cup of tea, Staff, while I have a word with David's father? Bless you.' I knew what that meant. The S.S.O. was unfailingly polite to women, and Mr. Fairbrother was about to get the rough side of his tongue. He had evacuated Mrs. Fairbrother before he brought in the big guns.

She sat quietly at the table while I made the tea. 'Father doesn't understand,' she apologised. 'It's because he's worried. You mustn't take too much notice of him.'

'I know,' I said. 'You're bound to be worried, both of you. Be odd if you weren't. Is David your only child—I can't remember?'

'Only natural one. We've two more, adopted. I couldn't have any more, after David. His father holds it against him, you know how men are? Thinks he nearly killed me.' She smiled gently. 'Poor boy, it wasn't his fault. Nurse, you *do* think we ought to let the doctor try, don't you?'

I wondered what I would do in her place. 'It's difficult for me to advise you,' I said at last. 'It's like this—they can't make him any worse; they may be able to help him. There's a chance, or Mr. Hutton wouldn't offer it to him.'

'That's what I mean. If it's only one chance in a million, we ought to let him have it. But Daddy seems to think that there isn't any chance, and that they're just—that they're experimenting on David. Practising, sort of.'

'No, that isn't true,' I said. 'It's an extremely difficult job, and they'd never even suggest it unless they thought it was worth while, and *would* give him an extra chance.'

'If he was your son, you'd let them try?'

I wished she wouldn't ask that. I wasn't old enough or wise enough to know. But I said: 'I'd trust Mr. Hutton to know what was right. He's a very good brain surgeon. I've worked with him, Mrs. Fairbrother, and I've never seen such painstaking work as his. I've never seen him make a mistake, either.' That was true enough. Mr. Hutton had his quota of failures, that was inevitable. But not through any fault of his, and never while I was in theatre. 'He has wonderful hands,' I told her.

She drank some tea and thought about it. 'That's good enough for me,' she decided at last. 'If anything—if we lost him, and they hadn't tried, I'd feel to blame ... Could I just peep at him, Nurse? I won't disturb him.'

I took her to look through the porthole. David was sleeping. I smiled. 'He looks like a little boy, asleep.'

'That's all he is, Nurse. Well, they never really grow up, do they? Look at Daddy—he's just a grown-up boy, that's all. He gets frightened. Men don't understand sickness, do they? It worries them. They think it might happen to them, too.'

It seemed to me that by the time the S.S.O. had finished talking to him, Mr Fairbrother would stand a good chance of understanding sickness, his son, himself, Mr. Rimbaud, and the S.S.O. as well. I said that I knew what she meant, and took her back to the kitchen. I went on plugging it into her how wonderful Mr. Hutton was for another five minutes before the men came out of the office. When they did I left the couple together and walked to the ward door with Mr. Verrier.

'That's that,' he said. 'They'll consent. Get 'em signed up before they go. Thanks, Staff. Oh, you can fix 'em with a lift home, can't you? No more buses at this hour. And if you can't, be sure to get in touch with me and I'll spring 'em a taxi.'

'I will,' I promised. I wondered how many senior residents, in how many hospitals, would have made such an offer. 'And——'

'Yes? Something bothering you, Staff?'

'On the contrary, I just wanted to congratulate you—on both counts. The consultancy as well as the engagement. May I?'

He smiled then, and all the tired lines round his eyes turned into laughter-lines. 'Well, bless you, Staff. She's told you, I take it?'

'Well, she just about managed to give me the report before she let it pop out! Everybody'll be frightfully pleased about it.'

'I'll tell you something, Staff. So am I. Good night.'

'Good night,' I said. '*Sir.*' Then I got through to the Casualty gate porter.

'Where do they want to go?' he asked.

I checked with the consent form on the desk. 'Half a minute . . . oh, Paradise Lane, Hall Green.'

He muttered something about its being a pity that they hadn't brought an angel to fly them back, and then told me to hold the line while he had a word with somebody. When he came back he said, 'There's a police car here, Staff. The driver says he'll drop them off, if they're ready. O.K.?'

'Great,' I said. 'Thanks, Bert. I'll send them straight over, shall I?'

'You do that. They'll see the car—in the O.P. park. The driver won't be two ticks—just getting an address.'

'Thank him, for Mr. Verrier, will you?'

The Fairbrothers were very grateful. 'Daddy' had subsided, and when he had signed the form and they were ready to go he asked me what size stockings Sister wore, which was a considerable change of tune. I didn't feel I could make the point that we weren't allowed to accept personal gifts. It would have been churlish, after his climb-down.

It was pretty quiet all night. Sister Caudle took Roberts away to run between Ward Five and Ward Six, and I didn't go to Meal at all but ate poached eggs in the kitchen. David woke screaming with fear and pain at four o'clock and I gave him the morphia right away and stayed with him until he went off again. The two sick nurses both slept until after six: Rogers wasn't too bad, but Sinji was making heavy weather of it. I don't suppose she was as used to the bug as we were. It had certainly hit her hard. She was so bubbly that I gave her a bed-rest, and told Rogers to keep after her to make her drink plenty. 'You're being barrier-nursed, you two,' I told them. 'So kindly *don't* go into the corridor, Rogers, even if you do feel well enough. You've got your own loo, through that door, and baths will have to wait. I've got a very sick boy, and I don't want him infected when he's due for anaesthetic. Right?'

Rogers said 'Yes, Staff,' and: 'No, Staff,' and: 'As if I would, Staff!' and look so cowed that I had to cheer her up by telling her about Sister Ross and the S.S.O. 'Bang goes another crazy dream,' she said. 'That's the last of the bachelors gone.'

'He's not a bachelor, Nurse Rogers, He's a widower. And he's not the last, by any means.'

'He's the last of the *mature* ones.'

'Well,' I said lightly, 'you can always set your cap at Dr. Ffestin-Jones. He won't see thirty-five again, if it's maturity you're after.'

Rogers sneezed several times, and then peered at me over her tissue. 'Get with it, Staff. He's got *children*. I ought to know—they go to my little sister's school.'

'Too bad,' I said. I got out of there quickly and stood scrubbing my hands outside for a long time. I remembered how his arm had flashed out to protect me, in the car. Of course. It was precisely the movement of a driver accustomed to carrying child passengers. And hadn't he said that it was habit? He had practically told me, only I'd been slow in the uptake.

I was still brooding on it at dinner, and in the end I asked Rose, 'Did you know that Dr. Jones had kids?'

'No. *Has* he? I thought he was a bachelor-man.'

'So did I, till someone mentioned his children.'

'Could be a widower, I suppose?'

'Could be,' I agreed. 'Like the S.S.O. But everybody knows about Mrs. Verrier having bulbar polio, and all that. Why, everyone told me when I first joined. But I've never heard very much about Dr. Jones.'

'That goes for me, too,' Rose said. 'Well, he isn't round the wards very much, like the others. And he's not very obtrusive, and he hasn't been here long. Lots of people don't even know him by sight. But I shouldn't really think there's a wife in the background, because——'

'Why not?'

I must have said it too quickly, because Rose stopped eating to turn and look me over. 'Oho? We're interested, are we?'

'Of course not, you muggins. I just wondered ... Well, *why* don't you think there's a wife in the picture?'

'Well, when they have the consultants' dinner-dance, after Christmas, they all bring their wives and concubines and things, don't they? And he and the S.S.O. always turn up solo. I know, because the residency maid told me. We had her up in Five while I was there, and she told me a lot of interesting little things. That was one of them.'

'Trust you to remember,' I said. 'And that reminds me— Geoff rang up last night, and I said I'd ring back this morning. He'll have had that registered parcel by now. Would you ring, if you were me?'

'No,' Rose said flatly. 'But you will. I can see it coming on. That's the trouble with you, Didi—you've got a non-conformist conscience, as somebody once called it.'

'Oscar Wilde, probably.'

'And Max somebody. Anyway, he reckoned it was the ruination of women, having it. You should watch it. You never know where it might lead you. You're just the sort who gets exploited. Dedication Jones is right, chum!'

I did ring, of course. I tried the site office first, and got no reply. Then I rang the house. Geoff's father answered. 'Thank God you've rung, Didi,' he said. His voice was louder than usual. 'I tried twice last night to get you—they wouldn't put me through. I should have thought that in the——'

'*You* rang?' That possibility had simply never occurred to me. 'But the man said—— But why? What's wrong?'

'You've not heard, then? Well, that's something. I wanted to tell you myself. It wouldn't——'

'Tell me *what*?' I said.

'Geoff's in the Queen's. Head injuries, and I don't know what else yet. I don't think they do, either.'

'Oh no! What was it—a car accident?' And if so, I asked myself, had it been my fault? Had it been a stress error, like Dennis O'Dea's? I felt terrible, nonconformist conscience or not. 'When?'

'Car? No. Beaten up, and pushed off a scaffolding.'

'He was *what*?' It sounded like a bad film.

'He went down to Charlecote Avenue with Mr. McKechnie, to look at the flooding. We're having a lot of trouble down there, and some of the residents are very worked up.'

'Yes, I know. Rose said there was something on the News.'

'That man Harris. He's started an absolute riot down there. And of course when they got the television cameras they went from bad to worse, showing off, you know. Harris and another man saw Geoff and Mr. McKechnie and egged the rest on to jostle them. So they climbed up on the staging of the new maisonettes at the end of the avenue. McKechnie managed to hang on until the police got to him, but Harris and his pals got hold of Geoff, and it ended with his being kicked in the head and booted off the cat-walk. Twenty feet up, he was ... They think his spine's injured, from what they say.'

I felt ice-cold. 'How is he now? What *do* they say at Queen's?'

'Critical, that's what I got on the phone. His mother's with him now. I think you'd better go, too. I've got a business to run somehow. You go, Delia.'

Frightened, I thought. Like little Mr. Fairbrother. 'Of course, I'll go this morning. Which ward?'

'He's in the—the unit, you know. Where they have the bad cases.'

'Intensive care?'

'That's it, yes.'

There was only one consolation in the whole sorry affair. Peter Ellis was in charge of Surgical Intensive. I should at least be able to get some information. Then I thought of something else. ' Mr. Lockyer, was there a registered letter for Geoff this morning?'

'Oh—yes, I did sign for something. Why?'

'Don't let it go to him. It's—actually it's my engagement ring, and——'

'Oh no, Delia! Not just now, surely?'

'No, not just now. Keep it safe somewhere.'

I didn't tell Rose. She was already in bed when I got to the flat, and I changed quietly and went out without disturbing her. I had to wait a long time for a bus, and I had plenty of opportunity for thinking. Only I couldn't. I felt paralysed, mentally. Everything was standing still, the way it does in the split second before two cars collide—if you happen to be an onlooker. But I wasn't supposed to be an onlooker. I was involved—yet I felt like a spectator. I suppose it was shock, really, but at the time I was shocked by the shock itself, by the fact that I had lost touch with my own emotions.

Geoff's mother was sitting in the bright little waiting-room of the intensive care unit, crying automatically. She looked as though she had been doing it for hours. When she saw me she cried all the more. A nurse brought us both some very good coffee and told me that I could look at Geoff in about five minutes. 'The doctor's with him at the moment,' she explained. 'But there isn't any real change.'

I put my cup down and followed her out into the corridor. 'I'd like to get a word with Mr. Ellis, if he's available,' I told her. 'He's a friend of mine. But on his own—away from Mrs. Lockyer.'

She looked doubtful until I explained that I was an S.R.N. from Teddy's. That made all the difference, as I'd known it would. 'Well, of course,' she promised. 'He's tied up this minute, but the minute he's free I'll come and get you. Who do I say?'

'Jones,' I said. 'Say it's Didi Jones. He'll know.'

Mrs. Lockyer looked up hopefully as I went in again. 'Have you seen him, Delia? How does he——'

'Not yet. You have, of course. How did he seem to you?'

'Terrible.' She began to cry again. 'He doesn't know me. And his poor face ... They kicked him, you know, those men. Did his father tell you? Hooligans! Nothing but hooligans.'

'Yes, they're pretty stirred up down there. It's understandable. You wouldn't like it. I'd feel like hitting somebody, too, if I were in their shoes.'

'But why Geoff? Why pick on Geoff? It isn't his fault. He can't help the flooding, can he? I mean, it's nature. It's an Act of God.'

I wasn't so sure about that.

After a while the same nurse put her head round the door and called me out with her eyes. 'The first cubicle,' she directed me. 'Not much to see, and he isn't conscious yet, but I know you want to look for yourself. Then Mr. Ellis'll see you. That's his room, over there. All right?'

'Thanks a lot,' I said. 'I'll only stay a moment, unless he comes round. If he does I'll call you.'

She was right. There wasn't much to see, in that glass box with its assorted shiny hardware and tubing. Most of Geoff's head was covered with bandages, and the one eye I could see was closed by a great pulpy bruise. The rest of him, naked under the single sheet, lay as flat and sunken as a typhoid. His breathing was very slow and shallow, and the monitor barely bleeped. Shock, I told myself. I watched the dark blood dripping steadily through its glass connection from the vacolitre on the bed's built-in hook overhead, and wondered just how much he had lost, how much they were giving. I spoke to him, but there wasn't any response. His hands lay flaccidly at his sides. Then I went out to see Peter.

He closed the door and gave me a chair. It was nice to see his gnomish grin again, and I said so. It warmed me a little.

'Nice to see you, too, Didi. I knew about you—his mother told me. Seemed to think I ought to draft you into Queen's to nurse him ... Yes, it's good to see you, but I wish the circs could have been different. Look, if you're this lad's fiancée I can talk freely to you, especially as you're S.R.N. I suppose you'll be expected to interpret to his family?'

'Something like that, yes. But he isn't——'

'Isn't what?'

'He isn't *exactly* my fiancé any more.'

'As of when, precisely?'

'Saturday,' I told him. 'And I sent his ring back to arrive this morning—but he hasn't received it, of course, so he's going to think—when he's able to think anything—that I probably didn't mean it, and that even if I did I'll revoke now.'

'Awkward, at this point,' Peter agreed.

'Very. Because when I stood in that cubicle just now, I didn't feel anything about him at all, except as a patient. And I know I ought to. That's why—— That's why I want you to give me something like a prognosis. I may have to adapt my thinking. Only there's a limit to the amount of unselfishness I'm capable of, if you see what I mean. If he was—— If he isn't going to do, then I've *got* to adapt, for his sake. If he is, it wouldn't be fair, once he's taken a grip on himself.'

'I know exactly what you mean. I wish everybody was as honest. And there's nothing more hurtful than being patronised by a sense of duty.'

'Just how bad *are* his injuries, Peter?'

Peter screwed up his face and turned the paperknife he was playing with from top to bottom a dozen times, before he spoke. 'Well, the head injuries . . . Only hairline fractures as far as we know. Could be brain damage—can't tell yet till the oedema resolves itself. A lot of laceration and bruising, of course. What we're most bothered about, actually, are possible spinal injuries. So far we've no reflexes below the third lumbar. I'm sure you get the picture?'

I did. We weren't talking about a man who might die, but about one who might be permanently paralysed below the waist, and who might have lesions that would make him no more than a vegetable, mentally. 'Yes, he could be paraplegic, permanently? Maybe dulled too.'

'Could be.' Peter looked up at me under his eyebrows without moving his head. 'Didi, you're not going to make the mistake of being swayed by false sentiment, are you? All very fine and dandy to hold back the ring hand-over ceremony . . . for the time being. Only don't, for God's sake, talk yourself into feeling that you'd be noble to tie yourself to someone you can't love, just out of—what? Pity? Don't do it, girl. It wouldn't be any kindness to him. And for you it'd be hell.'

'I don't know what I'll do. I have to wait and see how it goes. All I know is, I'm a *nurse*, Peter. I can't just walk out on him.'

'Not today, no. I appreciate that. I wouldn't let you, at this juncture, anyhow. But later on——'

'We don't know, do we? Whether he'll do?'

'True.'

'Peter, will you ring me when you know something more?'

'You bet your life I will. Be glad to. I'd have Rose on my tail if I didn't, wouldn't I?'

That reminded me. 'Thanks,' I said. 'Look, I believe you know my sister Freda.'

'Ah, the biologist? Yes. She's good fun.'

'I want to ask you an awfully personal question. You may think it's silly, but——'

'Ask away.'

'You're going to Canada, I believe. To British Columbia. Did you know Freda was going there, too?'

I needn't really have asked. 'You're joking! *Is* she? Well, there's a thing.'

'You didn't—— I mean, when did you decide?'

'Oh lord, ages ago.' He was too sharp not to get the message. 'Long before I met Freda, if that's what's on your mind. Surely not?'

'No, no, I just wondered.'

He put his head on one side and half closed his eyes. 'Just a minute, ducky. Does *Rose* think there's a connection? Is that what you're trying to break to me?'

'Something like that, yes. Only you're not to quote me. You won't, will you?'

'Wouldn't dream of it. But Rose—surely she realises that I want her to come too?'

I blinked at him. 'She doesn't realise anything of the sort! She thinks you're walking out on her, to be honest.'

Peter lay back in his chair, sighed, and looked up at the ceiling. 'Now just *how* did I manage to give that impression? I thought she sounded pretty chilly when I phoned her. But I took it that she suddenly didn't fancy Canada any more. And if she really couldn't face it, of course I'd be prepared to turn it down, even now.'

'Did you *tell* her that she was included?'

'Well, no! I assumed she'd naturally understand that. We should have to get married before we went, that's the whole point.'

'But you didn't actually *say* so?'

'I don't think I put it into words of one syllable, no.'

'If I were you,' I said, 'I'd sort it out sharpish. Before it bores into her. Before her next nights-off, too.'

He nodded. 'Received and understood. A darn good thing you *did* come here today. The chap upstairs does seem to take sledge-hammers to peanuts sometimes. Unfortunately.' He opened the door for me, and touched my shoulder as I passed him. 'Remember, Didi, no noble gestures. They're only a form of conceit, and they don't really help anyone.'

'I'll see,' I said. 'Thanks a lot, Peter.'

I didn't say much to Mrs. Lockyer about the possible paraplegia, or the brain damage. I just told her that nobody could really say anything at the moment. Geoff would have to be kept quiet, and we must all be patient. Then I said 'Now why not go home and get some sleep? By tonight he may be conscious.'

'No.' She tucked her chin into her coat collar. That meant she was going to be obstinate. Geoff had the same way of setting his jaw when he didn't want to be influenced. 'I shan't leave till his father can come. One of us must be here.'

'I'd stay myself,' I explained. 'But I have to go on duty tonight. We're far too short-staffed for me to ask for any nights-off. Besides, Geoff will need us more when he can talk.'

She peered down at her black court shoes. 'Is he going to die, Delia? You *would* tell me?' It took her quite a lot of effort to ask that.

Would I tell her? If I'd thought that, yes, I would. But I couldn't tell her the other possibilities, because I saw them as rather worse. So would she. 'Of course I don't think anything of the kind. Geoff's very tough. He's a strong boy. It would take more than Mr. Harris and his creepy friends to—to do that. Don't *worry*. Look, if you sit here worrying he may pick up your thoughts. Sick people do. Try to relax. He's getting the best possible attention, you know that.'

She didn't look too sure. 'What a pity they didn't take him to *your* hospital. You ought to be——'

'If he had been, I shouldn't have been allowed to nurse him. And we haven't a unit as good as this.'

'But *why* wouldn't they let you nurse him?'

'Because we never are allowed to nurse relatives, or close friends. They're pretty strict about that. Matron just won't hear of it. It's a good rule, too. You can't look after people properly if you're emotionally involved with them. It's no use to them.' Thinking back, it seemed to me that Peter Ellis had been saying that it was no use being uninvolved, either. Only I realised that there were ways and ways of being involved. 'You have to be detached, or it doesn't work.'

'I don't see that at all. Sick people *need* affection.'

She wouldn't understand. It was useless to argue with her. She knew about as much about psychology as I did about Pitman's shorthand.

It was Caradoc who handed over to me. Sister, he said, was off to her engagement dinner with Mr. Verrier. We had four more patients, all in Dr. Jones's beds, all for observation, and all completely without notes. There was sedation written up for them, and that was the lot. Dr. Jones still hadn't been in to see them, but he had rung to say that they were for psychotherapy and that all we had to do was to observe them, make notes of their conversation and behaviour, and report to him. 'I told him *we* weren't R.M.N.s,' Caradoc grumbled. 'Sister'll have a set of jugs when she finds out. He didn't send them in until after she'd gone off duty.'

'All at once? Are they transfers, then?'

'Yes, from some nursing home where he has beds, I take it.'

'So they're all p.p.s?'

'No. Just N.H.S. patients, he said.'

I frowned. 'I don't get it. But I suppose he'll explain when he comes. *If* he comes. Maybe Dr. Walsh'll see them?'

'No, it's his half day. *And* he's taken Nancy Serpell out with him. The story runs that they're going to plot the route of some car rally or other.'

'That young man certainly gets around,' I said. 'He asked me out, too. I never thought psychiatrists had so much initiative.'

Caradoc made a rude noise and took himself off. Little Nurse Hickin came bustling in as he went. 'Sorry I'm late, Staff. Old Mother Caudle sent me to Three, and then discovered you'd had an intake. Anything interesting?' She dumped her cape and came to read the report over my shoulder.

'Four for Dr. Jones,' I pointed out. 'Not for second opinions, just his own. Mrs. Berry, Miss Hughes, Mr. Flack, and Mr. Avon.'

'No diagnosis?'

'No. All for obs. He'll be down to see them later.'

'What about diet?'

'Oh, give them light, in the absence of any other instructions. And you've to keep your ears open, but not ask them any questions. Right?'

'Right.' She was reading the bit about David Fairbrother. 'Not so good, is he? Theatre Thursday. Wish I could see it done. I just never have the luck to see Mr. Hutton on the job.'

'He's a beautiful worker,' I said. 'But head things take such ages. It's tiring, in theatre. You seem to be standing there all day. And if you're not assisting you can't see much, really.'

'No, I suppose not. Well, I'll get on. Shall I see the new lot first, or do you want to?'

'You can ask about drinks,' I said. 'I want to look at Fairbrother first. By the way, barrier-nursing for those girls at the end. Let's not have anything go wrong now. In fact, you'd best not go in to Fairbrother at all, unless you're forced to. We can't be too careful.' I was trying to imagine his parents' reaction if, having given their consent, they had to wait for the operation much longer. 'It wasn't easy getting consent: let's not have the thing postponed now.'

I needn't have hurried to David. He was well sedated and fast asleep. He didn't wake when I tucked another blanket on to his bed. I saw that there was morphia checked off for six p.m. He wasn't likely to need more until after midnight.

Hickin called me into the kitchen as I passed, after waving to Rogers through the window. 'Staff, are those four p.p.s or not? He might have warned us, so that we could lay on the trimmings.'

'Caradoc Hughes said not. Specifically. Why?'

'Pretty demanding.' She picked up her notebook. 'Mrs. Berry—she wants a softer pillow, some Horlick's, some biscuits "in a little tin" in case she wakes, and where are her *green* pills? She's certainly not going to take these white things. Then there's Miss Hughes. Two hot water bottles, a thermos of very sweet coffee, and a better bedside lamp because the one she has is too bright. Mr. Flack always has Guinness last thing, and where's the "television lounge"? And Mr. Avon's just eighteen, crying his eyes out for his mum, and can't sleep in a room by himself. Oh, and he'd like some Bovril sandwiches and a cup of tea.'

I sighed. 'Well ... Horlicks, hotties, Bovril, and pillows. can do. Television lounges and Guinness are out. Avon can't share a room unless Dr. Jones says so, but I'll go and chat him up. That do you?'

'Right. And I don't like the look of Sinji. She looks as if she's cooking up a pneumonia. Lying on one side, grunting, blue round the mouth. I think you'd better take a look.'

'I was just going to, when you called me. She wasn't too good this morning. "Comfortable day" in the report means nothing. It's at night they show up in their true colours. I'd better start her on Terramycin—I can get Dr. Jones to write it up in retrospect.'

'I don't know how you dare! After all Tut tells us——'

'Time is of the essence, dear child,' I said. 'She's got to *have* an antibiotic, and the sooner the better. You should be commending me on my despatch. But that's not to say that *you* can get away with it. Not till you're registered, anyhow.'

She said that she wouldn't presume to prescribe, even then. That was what she thought. One day she would find herself rushing down a ward with a syringeful of coramine long before any doctor could get there, and saving a life. She would learn that rules have to be broken sometimes, I thought.

We had ironed out most of the difficulties by the time Dr. Jones came. He went in to see his people while I was on the phone answering enquiries, and I didn't see him for half an hour. When he did come to the office I queried their status. 'Nurse Hickin says they're so demanding she reckons they must be private patients. But they're not, are they?'

'Not now, no. Perfectly ordinary N.H.S. people.'

'You say "not *now*". You mean they have been?'

'Oh, didn't they tell you? They've all been in my nursing home beds, at Barnt Green. They can't afford it, but a lot of people dread a hospital. Well, a psychiatric hospital. So I let them stay there for a week or two, and then transfer them to a hospital as soon as they'll agree. Now that I've got these beds I saw no point in letting them empty their piggy banks any longer.'

'Couldn't you simply reduce their fees?'

'It isn't *my* nursing home. Matron is the proprietress, and gets her percentage. She feels the beds should go to fully paying patients, not to my waifs and strays. I'm hamstrung.'

'Look, none of us has done R.M.N. We don't know how to handle them, how to help them.'

'Just be nurses. Tender loving care. You know. Be good listeners. That's their crying need—somebody to *listen*. And when I say "listen", I mean listen uncritically. Make notes —for me—of any chats you have; be kind; accept them as they are.'

'They're not——'

'They're not psychotic, any of them. They're all affective conditions—what you'd call emotional difficulties. They won't act strangely, or do anything rash. They're not in the least out of touch with reality, they're simply ordinary people, over-reacting to stress. Does that help? Just be *calm*, that's the important thing.'

I said that we would try. Then I asked him to write up Sinji's Terramycin. 'Perhaps you'd like to look at her, too?'

He wasn't long in there. When he came back he said: 'True bill, Didi. Where's her case-paper?'

I handed it over, and told him how much I'd given. 'I know I should have waited,' I said, 'but the men don't usually mind if we get on and give things.'

'Hard drugs, too?'

'Oh no! Only in frantic emergency. Then anything goes. I mean, if the roof fell in on you now, and you screamed for morph., I'd probably give it to you and say you ordered it yourself.'

He smiled drily. 'I'm glad you wouldn't let a few regulations stand in your way if *I* were suffering. Nice of you!'

'You know what I mean. An emergency's an emergency.' The very word made me think of his emergency stop in the car, and then of the children Rogers had mentioned. Then I thought of Geoff. It was a train of thought I didn't quite understand, but there it was. I said, 'I was in the Queen's intensive this morning. Terribly well equipped, but so inhuman.'

'What were you doing there?' He gave me Sinji's notes back and looked up at me. 'Visiting the sick?'

'A man I—well, an old flame.'

'Warm enough still to rate a visit, though? You must have been engaged to him, surely, or they wouldn't let you in?'

'Yes, I was. Not now. At least——'

He stood up. He looked tired in the harsh light. 'I have to go over there tomorrow. Perhaps I could bring you a bulletin on him. What's his name?'

'Lockyer,' I said. 'Geoffrey Lockyer.'

He smiled faintly. I didn't know it then, but after that evening I wasn't going to see him smile again for quite a while. Not at me. And—though I didn't know that either—I was going to have nobody but myself to thank. But because I wasn't clairvoyant I relaxed and smiled back, and was moved by the shape of his head and the way his eyebrows precisely matched the double lift of his hairline. Then I brought my attention back to his voice. '. . . and that's your Miss Baxter's trouble,' he was saying. 'If they didn't keep taking the children away from her and into care, she wouldn't keep having more to replace them.'

'Do you think so? But she's too feckless not to.'

'She may not have any more chances. Miss Fantague wants to sterilise her, but I don't think I agree.'

'It's pretty irrevocable, isn't it?'

'Indeed. *We* can't predict what shape her future will take. She may marry, and want legal babies. Every woman has the right to that.'

'Yes, I'd think so if I were her, I suppose. Only I wouldn't have got into this muddle in the first place.'

'You're fond of children?'

I thought about his, wondered what they were and how old, and said: 'I've enjoyed nursing them. I'd be fond of my own, obviously. How do I know? I've never had any.'

'No. Unlike our Miss Baxter.' He smiled again, and as he passed me in the doorway he touched my bare forearm. I felt the down crackle with static the way a kitten's fur does. He didn't seem to notice. He just let his fingers run lightly down to my wrist and said: 'Good night, Delia.'

'*Nos da*,' I said foolishly. 'Is that right?'

His teeth gleamed in the dark corridor. 'That's right, *cariad*.' *Cariad*? It didn't sound like any of the things that a consultant should apply to a mere staff nurse.

I asked Nurse Thomas about it when she sat opposite to me at Meal. 'Literary or colloquial?' she wanted to know.

'Both,' I said. I wasn't going to be drawn like that.

'In writing, "beloved". But talking you'd use it for "Sweetheart", or "darling". Or to a lover. Or a child.'

I wondered just which way Dwyryd Jones had used it to me. As to a child, probably. Only that wasn't the way he had touched my arm. It still surprised me that there wasn't a red streak, like the track of a strep, running up my arm to tell the world what he had done to me.

CHAPTER EIGHT

As we left the dining-room on Wednesday morning, after night dinner, I ran into Alice Ratleigh on her way to the diet kitchen. She looked fine. Her face was still narrow, but colour improved it, and her eyes were bright. 'I'm glad to catch you,' I told her. 'I've another idea for you. Or rather, Rose Innes has. How about a Matron's job in a handicapped school, where you could have your brother with you?'

She was nodding before I had finished. 'Yes, that hit me, too. I've already applied. Pedworth Manor—they don't have many mongols: let's face it, most of them live happily at home—but there are a few.'

'Good,' I said. 'That's the stuff. And how's your mum?'

'Oh, they've operated. They reckon they've enucleated it completely. But I'm taking no chances. I'll accept the job, if I can get it, and then if anything does go wrong it'll all be so much simpler. And it's no further from home than Teddy's is.'

I wished her luck, and hurried on to catch up with Rose. She'd been late off duty, and for once we hadn't been sitting together to exchange gossip. 'That girl looks a whole lot better,' she commented. 'Not that I could ever really like her, but this last month or two she's been quite unbearable —bossy, self-centred, full of moans. You'd think nobody else had problems. Still, she's all right now ... That's *her* settled. How about you?' She was looking at me as though she wanted to get me ticked off on some list before she went on to another patient. 'Any news of Geoff?'

'Oh, I must ring up ... No, I'll go over to Queen's.' I wondered whether I looked as guilty as I felt. Rose didn't miss much. 'Funny, for a moment I'd clean forgotten all about him! Just how stupid do we get on nights? It dulls the brain or something.'

Rose looked abominably pleased with herself. 'Ah, a lot of funny things happen on nights. Don't you want to know what happened to *me* last night?'

'What did?'

'I had a proposal. How about that, then?'

'Of marriage, I trust?' I said.

'But of course! From Peter. He rang up. Gosh, there was old Caudle right behind me, and I didn't even care. When I put the phone down, she——'

'What did he *say*, for heaven's sake? And what did you say?'

'Well, he said *we'd* have to get married before *we* went to Canada, and how did I feel about three weeks on Saturday. So I said: "*We*? I didn't know I was included, and marriage has never even been mentioned." That seemed to baffle him a bit—but honestly, he's never actually *said* anything. The idiot! Anyhow, there I was——'

'But did you say "yes"?'

She widened. 'Naturally! What else could I say? So you will be my bridesmaid, won't you? I'll stand you a super dress. Just a quiet do, but we must have it at St. James's, because Peter's uncle's the vicar and he wants him to marry us. It's not so bad inside: the stained glass is nice, even if the outside's falling apart ... Oh, I could hug all the policemen this morning. I could *run* all the way to the flat, even if my feet are killing me!'

We didn't run, I hadn't any run left in me, but she did have the occasional skip round a lamp-post along Hagley Road. When we did get home there was an *Interflora* van pulling up outside. 'For you,' I predicted. 'A dozen red roses. Want to bet?'

She waited at the gate until the van driver came to her. Yes, she was Miss Innes, she said. Then she came in positively giggling, which is a thing she doesn't normally do. 'Wrong again,' she told me. 'Two dozen. And aren't they beauties? The real old red rose smell—not like some of these modern horrors, all shape and no scent.' Upstairs she took them out of their cellophane and found the card tied to them. She burst out laughing. 'Look at that! *Go on, meanie, give some to Didi*. Typical. How unromantic can men be? Anyhow, I was going to give you half to take to Geoff.'

'He wouldn't even notice them, my dear. And I certainly wouldn't take half.'

'Well, look, put six in your room, six in mine, six in the sitting-room, and you take six to Ma Lockyer. Fair?'

'And just what do we use for vases? We've only one that's tall enough. Why not put them all in the sitting-room when we're up, and in your room when you go to bed? It's the reverse of the usual practice, but does that matter?'

She still insisted that I took half a dozen with me. It was too silly, taking flowers into an intensive care unit—as silly as taking them into theatre—so I left them on the window-sill in the corridor at Queen's, until I could decide whether to give them to Mrs. Lockyer or the nurse. That decided itself: Mrs. Lockyer wasn't there. Her husband was in the waiting room, talking gloomily to another man who drifted out as I went in. He looked about as pleased to see me as he would be to find dry-rot in his bathroom. Geoff had been conscious, briefly, he told me, but only long enough to open one eye and move his fingers. 'Is that good?' he wanted to know. 'Does it mean he'll be all right?'

'It's an improvement, anyway,' I assured him. 'But it *is* going to be a slow business. We'll have to be very patient. You're not going to see changes overnight.' I felt as though I were on duty, talking to a patient's relatives. I could hear the awful professional neutrality in my voice, the detachment, the calm and confident tone, and all the rest of the things we were taught, and I felt mean. 'Try not to fret, Mr. Lockyer.'

'Fret? Perhaps it's a good thing he *isn't* conscious! At least he can't read the papers.' He turned to snatch up the *Post* from his chair. 'At least he can't see *this*.' He smacked the front page with the back of his hand and thrust the paper at me.

There was a headline: FLOOD DAMAGE—WHOSE FAULT? *Tenants Stage Protest March.* There was a photograph, too, of Mr. Harris and a lot of other people carrying banners reading: *Who skimped the job?* and: *We demand action*, and: *Action now on floods.* The council's tenants in Charlecote Avenue, the report said, were demanding compensation for ruined carpets and furniture, and for personal inconvenience. Council officials were denying responsibility, and a spokesman had said that their surveyor was not satisfied with the way the drainage work had been carried out. He had called the contractors to meet him so that the whole question could be thrashed out. He had advised the council against paying any compensation until this had been done. And so on. And police had been drafted in from other areas to keep public order, since feelings were running very high . . . I could sympathise.

I read it through twice before I looked up. 'Does this mean that they're blaming you? B.R. and L.?'

'It means they're blaming that boy in there.' He jerked his big thumb towards the cubicles. 'Geoff. That's who they're blaming. He did the quantities and the levels for that job, didn't he? And if there's anything wrong, then McKechnie's in it too. Isn't he? But you just watch master McKechnie duck out and leave Geoff to hold the baby!'

So everything Father had said was true. Bright, Richards, and Lockyer were just as capable of fiddling their contract work as Grafton and Chelwood were. There didn't seem to be any right thing to say. 'But at least they can't drag Geoff off to this enquiry.'

'No.' He thumped his chest angrily. 'But they can drag *me* there, can't they? I'm responsible, in the end. *I* have to carry the can, don't I?'

'Why shouldn't Mr. McKechnie help to carry it, too?'

'I'd need evidence, wouldn't I? McKechnie looks after himself. Like he did with that house he promised me.'

'What house? You don't mean the one——'

'The one Geoff wanted for you two. Guerdon Road. He took you to see it, didn't he? Well, you can say goodbye to that. It was all cut and dried—but somebody offered him more money and he called it off.' He snapped his fingers. 'Just like that! Do you think promises mean anything to *him*?'

It occurred to me that Geoff might have rejected it, that Saturday evening, when they had been expecting the McKechnies in for drinks. I wanted to say, too, that I was glad Geoff wasn't still lumbered with it, but it wasn't the time to remind his father that our engagement was off, and that I had no official reason for visiting Geoff at all. 'I'm so sorry,' I said lamely. 'I thought you and the McKechnies were good friends.'

'Friends?' Mr. Lockyer laughed shortly. 'Just because

people mix with us socially, it doesn't mean they're *friends*. In business you have to cultivate a lot of people you wouldn't otherwise give house room to . . . Well, talk of the devil!' He was looking out through the glass panel in the door.

'What's wrong?' I said. I couldn't see past his square head.

'Talk of McKechnie, there's that girl of his. What's her name, now? Isobel, that's it. She must have come to see Geoff. I suppose her father sent her, to see what she could find out. Damned nerve!'

I began to feel distinctly cross with Mr. Lockyer, and I warmed towards Isobel correspondingly. 'Let me pass, please,' I said. 'I'd like to see her. She *could* have come because she likes Geoff, not because anyone "sent" her.'

He moved aside reluctantly. 'They haven't let her go in, anyhow.' He looked so triumphant that I felt like hitting him. As it was he moved back sharply, otherwise the doorknob would very likely have winded him.

Isobel had moved fast. She was already at the other end of the long corridor, but she stopped and turned round when she heard me clicking away behind her. She looked puzzled until I reached her. Then she blushed, and said: 'You're Delia, aren't you? I've seen your photograph at the Lockyers' house. I didn't—well, I didn't think you'd be here.'

'And you're Isobel. I saw yours in the *Mail*. I didn't expect to see you, either. I suppose they didn't let you see Geoff?'

'Well, no. They said was I a relative or anything, and I'm not. So I just saw him from the door, sort of.'

'He isn't properly conscious,' I consoled her. 'He most probably wouldn't know you.'

'No, so they said. They—the nurse said his condition was "still rather critical". Does that mean——'

I wished, not for the first time, that my profession was allowed a larger vocabulary, instead of being tied to all those carefully graded phrases ranging from *extremely critical*, through *satisfactory* to *quite comfortable*. After all, people who were satisfactory and comfortable oughtn't to be in hospital at all, from the lay viewpoint. And it was obvious that things were critical if a patient landed in an intensive care unit. I remembered being checked by Matron on one occasion when she had heard me tell an enquiring relative: 'He's marvellous today—he's even sitting up and washing his own feet.' Apparently I should have said that the recovering polio patient was 'fairly comfortable'. To my mind it meant far more to his mother to know that he was mobile and cheerful, and his feet were a private joke between us anyway, but Matron would never have understood that.

'It just means,' I explained, 'that they can't be quite sure just how it'll go or how long it'll take for him to improve.'

She was a very pretty girl, even with tears sliding down her pink cheeks. With eyes as blue as that she could even cry decoratively. 'Oh God,' she said. 'He won't *die*, will he? I need to know. Please tell me. You're a nurse.'

She really meant it, I could see that. And she could take it, the way she was feeling. So I held her gaze and said it straight out. It was the only fair thing to do. 'No, I don't think he'll die, Isobel. But that fall didn't do him any sort of good. Especially his spine. He could be paralysed, possibly permanently. His legs, anyhow. And there's just a chance that he may be a bit—well, confused, mentally. But I think his skull has survived the booting pretty well, because he did open his eyes and move his hands this morning, his father tells me. So I wouldn't dwell too much on that aspect. But you do have to face it that he *may* have to live in a wheelchair.' I put my hand on her wrist to tell her I was still there. 'Do you understand?'

'Yes.' She began to see me again. 'But that isn't so important.'

'No?' I was wondering whether her finishing school had forgotten to tell her about the birds and the bees. 'He might not be a—a complete man, as it were.'

She blushed again. 'I meant relatively. It's better to be alive in a wheelchair, with incapacities, than not to be. Isn't it? And the physical isn't everything.'

'It is to a man,' I said. Then I took a chance. 'Isobel, are you in love with Geoff?'

She didn't need to say it. Her face was enough. All the same, she managed a nod.

'Because if you are, don't be afraid to tell me, or him. I broke off our engagement last Saturday. Or did you know?'

'He—he said you'd quarrelled. He didn't say the engagement was definitely off. And when I saw you here, I thought——'

'That it was on again? No, I was simply doing the decent thing. I didn't want him to feel deserted, just at this point. It would have been cruel to stay away.'

'That was good of you.'

'No, not good. Actually it was fairly automatic. It comes of being a nurse, I suppose. I'm not in love with Geoff. I don't even like him very much, to be absolutely truthful. I'm glad you do. He needs somebody, only not me. I'm just not his sort. Good luck, Isobel.'

'Thank you,' she said. 'And if he does come to, will you tell him I came?'

'Of course. And come again. I'll try and fix it so that they let you in instead of me. All right?'

She leaned forward quickly and kissed my cheek. She smelt of *Prétexte* and I could guess just who had given it to her. It was probably the only decent perfume he'd ever heard of. I wanted to cry too, just for a second. It was the complete and classic handover.

I didn't go into the waiting-room again. I hung around until the nurse I'd met came along and told me I could look at Geoff. He was breathing better, and they'd taken him off the drip. There was still no response when I spoke, but his hand moved when I touched it, and I thought it tightened a little on my fingers. Beyond that, nothing. I told the nurse so outside.

'But he's done better than that,' she said. 'He opened his eyes when his father spoke to him. And when I was talking to that young woman—Miss McKechnie, is it?—he lifted one hand, as if he could hear her voice. I just let her stand by the door, you know. She didn't go in.'

She seemed a reasonable girl. 'Look,' I said, 'if I were to stop coming, would you let her in instead?'

'Well, if she isn't——'

'His fiancée?'

'Yes. Or a relative.'

'Actually she's nearer to it than I am. I broke it off just before this happened. But they won't have told you so—his mother doesn't know yet.'

'I see. And she's—your successor?'

'Sort of,' I said. 'I think she'd like to be.'

'And what would *he* like?'

'Who knows? I think they're very well suited. She's a lot more—pliable than I am. And resilient.'

'Even if——?'

'Even if,' I said. 'She's a nice kid, and she's in love with him. He needs someone like that. Someone who'll devote herself.'

She thought I was mad, but she smiled in a baffled kind of way. 'Oh well, it's your life. Yes, I'll let Miss McKechnie in next time, if that's the way it is. It might just help him.'

'In that case,' I mentioned, 'there are half a dozen red roses for you out in the corridor. Don't put them in Mr. Ellis's room—he paid for them.'

That really did fox her. She was still watching me when I turned round at the far end. Still, she did wave.

I told Rose about Isobel when we were getting ready to go on duty that night. I also told her about Mr. Lockyer, and the kerfuffle in the *Post* about the flooding. And she, too, remembered what Father had told us about Grafton and Chelwood, and about B.R. and L. too. 'I begin to think you're well out of that set-up,' she said. 'You're not the sort for intrigue. *I'd* be better at it than you, not that I'd want to be. It smells, doesn't it?'

'I'm afraid it does. But I still feel like a rat deserting the sinking ship, somehow.'

'Then don't. There's one thing, though——'

'What?'

'Look, if the McKechnie girl's getting involved with Geoff, *she* isn't going to let Daddy put him in bad with the council, is she? If she's got any influence with him at all, and most girls have with their fathers. Especially the sort whose fathers spend money on Swiss finishing schools.'

I hadn't thought of that. 'Clever,' I said. 'It takes you to see these points.'

'That is, if Daddy *knows*.'

'He soon will,' I told her. 'Mind you, I don't want to deflect the sword of justice, but I'm quite prepared to ring up Mr. Lockyer and make the point to him. He's got enough sense to use the information, I should think.'

'Mightn't that make trouble for little Isobel?'

'I doubt it. She's got quite a strong chin. And again, McKechnie may even be pleased. It puts one contractor securely in his pocket. It cuts both ways, doesn't it? They can blackmail one another. Only, if it turns out badly, he may not want his daughter to marry a paraplegic.'

'The McKechnie type is so commercial, Didi. To them a paraplegic is one thing, a rich paraplegic is another, and they'd sacrifice their daughters to Old Nick himself if he happened to be a profitable contact. If you see what I mean.'

I did, I said. Not that I saw Isobel exactly as a girl about to be sacrificed, but that wasn't the point.

When I rang, on the way to Teddy's, Mrs. Lockyer answered. She said: 'Daddy's gone back to the Queen's, dear. I've been there most of the day. Did you see Geoff this morning?'

I said yes, and that I thought he was improving. Then I added: 'Isobel McKechnie was there, too.'

'*Was* she? Oh, how nice of her. She seems very taken with Geoff, doesn't she?' It seemed to me that Mrs. Lockyer sounded distinctly taken with Isobel.

'Very,' I said. 'Oh, yes, she's very fond of Geoff. I expect that's why she went—though Mr. Lockyer seemed to think her father had sent her.'

She sounded thoroughly disconcerted then. 'But—but you don't seem to *mind*, Delia.'

'Look,' I said, 'there are a lot of things I haven't told you. I thought you had enough problems at the moment. But maybe I'm one of them. You've never really ... Well, forget about that. When Mr. Lockyer comes in will you tell him that I rang, and that I said I wouldn't be wanting that registered parcel back? He'll know what I mean. Maybe Isobel would like it.'

She was flustered now. 'Parcel? *Registered* parcel, dear? I don't know what parcel you mean.'

'Mr. Lockyer knows,' I told her. 'He'll explain. I have to rush now—I'm due on duty.'

Rose had been leaning against the door, listening. When I put the receiver down she said: 'That's telling her.'

'The nearest I could get. Mrs. L. only sees what she wants

o see. And once she sees Isobel as a match for Geoff she won't rest until she's got them well and truly married off. She'll waste no time grieving about *me*. She thinks nurses are "common". Isobel is far more like her image of a wife for Geoff.'

'Hm. If—and when—he's able to marry anybody at all.'

'Yes, if and when. But I don't feel as anxious about him as I did. I mean, if he was a patient, I'd know. And I know about him. He'll do all right, I'm sure.' It wasn't Geoff I was anxious about; it was something—or someone—else, only I couldn't place it. 'I *do* usually know, don't I?'

'Oh yes, your hunches usually are right,' Rose allowed. 'I've never known you wrong yet about a dicey patient. You had a hunch about that peritonitis boy when the S.S.O. had given him up, didn't you? Remember?'

I remembered. I had disobeyed every order the S.S.O. had given that night—but Micky Langtry was still alive because of it. Or the S.S.O. had been generous enough to say so. 'Yes, Micky. And I've got one now, about Iso, only I don't know which of them it is.' I wasn't exaggerating. The nearer we got to Teddy's the worse it was. I had geese walking over my grave in all directions by the time we were taking off our coats. 'Maybe Tony Sugden's in again?' I mused. 'Lord, I do hope not. He's had enough.'

Rose came away from the mirror still pinning her cap to her front hair. 'Ah, I knew I had something to tell you. About Tony. I hear he's got that Bache child spending her sick-leave at his place. Quick work!'

'Who told *you*? You hear far more than I ever do.'

Rose grinned. 'It's a long story. Bache is cousin to Peggy Brown, in Six, and told her. Peggy told Andy Gilpin—because he'd spotted Bache as soon as she joined, and you know what he is about baby-faced blondes. So Peggy twitted him about her and told him he'd got competition. Then Andy told me, and asked me who Tony was. There you are. It's simple, if you keep your ears open.'

'Poor little Bache,' I said. 'I hope she's in the picture. About Tony, I mean.'

'Well, *I* hope she *isn't*. Let her be happy for a while. She lost one boy-friend, apparently, about a month ago. He was run over by a lorry, right in front of her, Peggy says. Ran across his kidneys.'

'Tough,' I said. 'Oh, hence the renal colic? I wonder if Dr Jones knows?'

'Possibly. Hysteria's a pretty funny thing. You know we're lucky, having chaps who want us and who don't have obstacles all round them.'

'Speak for yourself,' I said. 'Me, I'm very much a single lady at the moment.'

'Rocky Walsh notwithstanding?' She was joking.

'Not my type,' I said. 'Not for going out with. At least I don't think so. Too stimulating.'

'Ah, you prefer the Celtic Twilight? I know darn well you're carrying a torch for somebody. Is that it?'

'Could be,' I said. 'Do come on—we'll be late for breakfast.'

In the dining-room she asked again, '*Is* that it?'

I remembered my last meeting with Dwyryd Jones and sighed. 'I daren't even think about it. It makes me feel incoherent.'

'That's a sure sign,' said Rose. 'I feel just the same myself if I dwell on Peter. I keep thinking I'll wake up and find I invented him.'

I knew what she meant. 'Me too. Only I'd hate him—or anyone else—to know. And anyway, I couldn't possibly invent anyone half as dishy.'

'You think he *won't* know? I thought psychiatrists could read people like books.'

I said I hoped he couldn't, for he'd be bored to tears by the time he'd got as far as Chapter Two.

Sister Ross was shut in the office with the S.S.O. when little Hickin and I went on duty. So I told Serpell and Robson to clear off, and Hickin and I prowled up and down the corridor until they emerged. I was still uneasy about something, but everything looked normal enough. Then Hickin, on her toes to reach the porthole, said: 'Has Rogers gone back to the Home, then? There's only one of them here now ... Oh no, Rogers is here. Sinji isn't.'

I came to check for myself. Then I heard: 'Staff Nurse Jones!'

I turned round. 'Yes, Sister?'

'Why didn't you tell me it was after half past, you wretched girl? You know there's no clock in the office, and you know how accurate my watch is.'

I looked at the S.S.O. loping along the path outside. 'I didn't want to interrupt, Sister.'

'I'll bet you didn't! Come along, then. I don't want to be here all night.' She looked pink and happy, and I was glad. It was nice to see other people's affairs going well, even if my own came apart in my hands. 'Those four of Dr. Jones's,' she began. 'I can't imagine what he's led them to expect, but *really*!' She pushed her hair back and blew a silent whistle. 'They're the end!'

'I know,' I said. 'I had some last night. They'll settle down, given time. It must be quite a change from a private home.'

'Well, Dr. Jones spends hours with them. Literally. He must have more patience than I have. At any rate, there's nothing to report about them. They're alive and kicking, and there our concern ends. I'm told that their notes—except any we write—are completely confidential. Fair enough, but I feel a bit shut out. Don't you?'

'Yes and no,' I said. 'I'd be interested to know how they tick. On the other hand, if I were one of them I wouldn't want my private affairs being discussed by the nurses.'

'It would depend on the nurses.'

'And on the affairs,' I said. 'Now, about David. What sort of prep do they want? Mr. Hutton isn't always consistent.'

'There's nothing for you to do except stop his breakfast. I've shaved his head and all that. Well, I had some expert help.' The S.S.O., I decided, certainly had to be in love if he would so far climb down from his lordly status as to shave the head of a mere patient, or even to watch someone else doing it. 'He can have drinks up to four o'clock, but frankly I'm hoping he won't wake for them. That way he won't even know he's going to theatre. We've not told him yet, anyhow. But if he does wake, enough to find he's shaved, you'll have to break it gently.'

'Yes, Sister. And Miss Baxter?'

'Oh, she's fine. There you are, you see. Dr. Jones goes in and spends half an hour or so with her, then out he trots and that's that. She says she understands her backache now, and she knows she won't get it any more! It's Greek to me.'

'Yes, he has theories about her,' I said. 'He says Miss Fantague wants to sterilise her.'

'Yes. And she's going to.'

'Oh? I thought Dr. Jones didn't agree?'

'No, dear, but Miss Baxter does. If you ask me, *that's* what's cured her backache—the prospect of being able to live it up and not produce any more little *illegitimae*. Not Dr. Jones, at all.'

That struck me as very funny. 'Don't *tell* him so, Sister. He sees her as the great earth-mother who needs children round her skirts to be happy. She must have been stringing him along.'

'Which is an occupational risk, presumably. Oh, I'll let him keep his illusions. But she's going back to Five tomorrow, for Miss Fantague's Friday list. Now, who else?'

'Nurse Sinji?' I suggested. 'She seems to have been moved.'

'Ah, yes, poor child. I asked the S.M.O. to come to her this morning—she looked ghastly, and her pulse was simply running. Well, he flew into an absolute fury, and transferred her up to Dr. Watterson's sideward straight away. She deteriorated so fast! But there was no need for him to be quite so rude. And noisy.'

'To you, Sister?'

'Not *to* me, no. Just at the air, generally. He hardly spoke to me at all. I've been told nothing. But I gathered from the remarks flying around that she needed "more specialised care than this madhouse can give her". Charming!'

'She had pneumonia. Why move her? *That* wouldn't help!'

'Oh no. It was "far worse than pneumonia", and why hadn't he been fetched before. And so on.'

The hunch was now right on the top of everything else in my head. 'That was my fault, Sister. I'm so sorry. But there didn't seem much sense in fetching him out in the night, to a plain classic pneumonia. Not when Dr. Jones was here on the spot.'

'I quite agree, Staff. I'd have done the same myself. He'd have been even more furious if you *had* got him up—you know how he goes on about his insomnia. He'd have said why didn't you get the houseman.'

'Dr. Hastri and Miss Sadler do enough overtime as it is.'

'Exactly. Never mind, the wretched man's leaving soon. Retiring, rather. Something wrong with a man who's still a house officer when he's at retiring age, if you ask me. Rogers is a lot better. Still a raised temp, though, so not to get up yet except for a bath. Is there anything else I ought to tell you?'

'The Avon boy, Sister. He doesn't like being alone. Is he more settled? He's awfully emotional.'

'Ah yes. He's quite O.K. if we leave his door ajar. Shut it, and all hell breaks loose. Leave the light well up at his end of the corridor, when you dim down the others, will you?'

'I'll do that . . . Nobody much to do rounds tonight, then? The S.S.O. won't want to see David again. Dr. Jones has been, and——'

'He's been here half the day. But that doesn't by any means guarantee that he won't be here half the night as well.' I rather hoped she was right. 'I've done my stint, anyway. Good night, Staff.'

'Good night, Sister,' I said. 'Steady as you go through the shrubbery.'

Rogers couldn't enlighten me about Sinji, either. 'It was all so quick,' she said. 'One minute the S.M.O. was here blowing his top, the next she'd been whipped away. Mind, she was ill. All that swelling. It—well, you couldn't see her eyes at all.'

I frowned. '*Swelling?* What sort of swelling?'

'What's it called. Angio-something?'

'You mean angioneurotic oedema?'

'That's it, yes. And she was squealing with pain.'

'But surely Sister saw her?'

'Oh yes, but it came up so suddenly, even after she'd sent for the S.M.O. it got worse. Odd, wasn't it?'

'Very odd,' I agreed. And I wondered why Sister hadn't mentioned it. The hunch was still with me, so it evidently didn't have any connection with Sinji. There was trouble still to come.

Dwyryd Jones did come down, not half an hour after

Sister had gone. That was as far as it went. He didn't speak to me. He walked straight through to the Avon boy's cubicle, stayed about ten minutes, and then stalked right past the office door. I thought he must have gone to see Miss Baxter, but when I got up to look he was already outside on the path, with his head turned well away from the ward windows. He couldn't possibly have missed seeing me in the office—the door had been wide open, so that I could see and hear everything that went on in the unit. It was the cut direct, and it was more than I could bear. I had a private weep in the sluiceroom before I went to look at Miss Baxter.

'Work that one out,' I told Rose at Meal. 'So much for all his sweet talk about bringing me a bulletin on Geoff, and all the rest of it.' I pushed my plate away. 'D'you know, it's quite killed my appetite.' Actually I wanted to cry again, but it wasn't the time or the place, and Rose would have thought it pretty childish too, to say nothing of the fifteen or so night juniors at the next table.

'Poor old thing! Well, indeed, let's work it out. You've obviously got his goat somehow, but how? Think.'

'I've *been* thinking. I've thought myself dizzy.'

'Maybe he did go to Queen's. And maybe Peter told him that you and Geoff were solidly engaged.'

'No, Peter knows it's off. I told him.'

'Could he have found out that Geoff's going to turn him out of his flat? He'd naturally think you were in it too, if——'

'No, it can't be that. Because Mr. Lockyer didn't get it after all. McKechnie promised it to him, and then said he'd had a better offer, and called it off.'

'Naughty ... Well, have you been telling anyone how you feel about him? Maybe it's got back, and the dear man's embarrassed. It can happen, on this grapevine. Don't I know it.'

'Only you,' I said. 'Have you told anyone?'

'Of course. I gave it to the B.B.C., the *Post*, the *Mail*, half the theatre porters, and Matron. What do you think?'

'Sorry. Then what *can* it be?'

'Ah, men tick in strange ways, lovey. Could be it wasn't you he was wild with at all. He could have been preoccupied with something entirely different. Heaven knows, I've walked past folk myself when my mind's been busy. Yes, perhaps he was just deep in thought, and next time you meet everything'll come up roses, as they say.'

'He didn't *look* deep in thought. He simply looked ... oh, cold and distant. Back like a ramrod, all that.'

'Now that's something I *do* know about psychology. Peter told me that if people walk about with ramrod backs, all *consciously* upright, it's because somebody has suggested that they're not. So they have to prove it. The way incompetent people are always terribly bossy, just to try to prove that they can control things.'

'Maybe that's why Geoff is always so consciously virtuous—because his little fiddles won't stand investigation?'

'Could be, yes.'

'Wait!' I said. 'Is it possible that Rocky Walsh is at the bottom of it? That he's said something to upset him?'

'Such as?'

I tried to remember exactly what we'd talked about. Geoff, making decisions, and being low-spirited mostly. Hadn't he said that girls under twenty-five only got depressed if they were either psychotic or crossed in love? And I'd cried. 'He could have said I'd cried on him.'

'And did you?'

'Not literally. In his presence, yes. Three yards away, at a rough guess. But he could have exaggerated.'

'And that would cause this Jones to go all upstage?'

'It might.'

'Then he must be potty. Unless, of course, he has evil designs on you, and sees all these Lockyers and Walshes as too much bodyguard?'

'He couldn't be so childish!'

'All men are childish, old dear. Even my nice Peter is at times.' She smiled. 'Perhaps the secret police of *Plaid Cymru* have ordered him to break off diplomatic relations with the enemy?'

Rose wasn't helping. I was still worried. I still had the nagging hunch that something, somewhere, was wrong, and that it concerned me. Horribly wrong. The stupid thing was that I'd had all the facts given to me on a plate, if I'd only realised it, and ought to have been able to put my finger straight on to the answer. But I didn't, and I couldn't. Why,

I shall never know, except that night-duty is a muddling thing to adjust to, and on top of that I'd used up quite a lot of emotional energy, one way and another. I suppose it all helped to blur my judgement.

CHAPTER NINE

IF I had ever doubted Tut's assertion that low spirits mean low resistance to infection, and in fact I hadn't, it would have been amply proved to me next day. Instead of going on duty, I found myself being trundled along in a wheel-chair by Sister Pipe, immediately—or so it seemed—after walking into the dining-room for night breakfast. I gathered later that I had passed out as I approached the hot-plate and had been an unconscionable time in reviving.

'You're a nice one!' Home Sister was saying. 'Fancy coming on duty with a temperature like that! You should have stayed at home, but now you're here you can just go to bed in Isolation, madam.'

I felt too ill to tell her that I'd never been aware of running a temperature, that I hadn't felt more than tired and a little giddy—which I put down to an almost sleepless day—and that Iso was the last place I wanted to go to. She tucked me into bed opposite Rogers, and Caradoc came in with a jug of lemonade and said: 'What are you?' After that it was just a long hot, cold, sweating, shivering, oddly-peopled dream until I woke up and found Rose leaning on the bottom rail on my bed with a feeding-cup in her hand.

'That's better,' she said. 'And about time, too.'

I looked at her, and the window, and then the room. Rogers wasn't there any more, and her bed was made up. 'When did Rogers go?' I said. 'I didn't hear a thing.'

'Last Friday. Want some tea?'

That was just silly. 'Look, she was here when——'

'That, my poor mixed-up kid, was nearly a week ago.' Rose said calmly. It just didn't seem possible, and I said so, but she simply fed me tea and assured me: 'It's not only

131

possible, it's perfectly true. It's seven o'clock, Thursday morning, and all's well.'

I tried to sit up, felt far too wobbly, and lay down again. Thursday. *Last* Thursday. 'Fairbrother?' I said. 'Is he——'

'Holding his own. Very quiet, not in any pain, just a bit dazed. They think he'll do.'

'I'm glad. And Sinji?'

Rose sighed. 'Look, everyone's fine. It's you I'm concerned about—not David, or Sinji, or anyone else. The rot you've been talking! No wonder they sent *me* down here to relieve—I was astounded that Matron didn't forbid me the area for five miles round Iso. You know what she is.'

'What have I been talking about?'

'What haven't you? If it's any comfort to you, they said you didn't do it in the daytime. I've had nothing but Dwyryd, Dwyryd, Dwyryd; and Dwyryd's children, his flat, his ox, his ass, and his maidservant, *ad nauseam*. Talk about a one-track mind!'

'Oh no, don't pull my leg, Rose! I feel awful.'

'Well, not quite as bad as that. But it was a good thing he wasn't here. He'd have got swelled head. It's a dispensation of providence that he's away, if you ask me.'

'Away? Where?'

'In his native land of song, I assume. "Home" was what he told the gatehouse men when he shook the dust. The morning after he gave you the brush-off. Or the 'flu.'

School holidays, perhaps, I thought. But the date hadn't been on the list in the front office when I'd checked once. I wished Rogers could be there: she was the only one who could tell me some of the things I needed to know. 'I wish Rogers was here.'

Rose's eyebrows shot up. 'For why? *You* wanting to share a room? And with a first-year? You know how you'd hate it.'

'Something I wanted to ask her.'

'Yes I know what, too. That much emerged from your viral ravings. And I know the answer. Will you be good and go to sleep again if I tell you?'

'Yes. But how did you find out?'

'I asked Rogers, dear. Simple. All right?'

'All right,' I said.

'Lie down, then ... That's better. Well now, they're

twins, aged eight, and their names—if it's to be believed—are Catrin and Mair. Catrin's pony-mad, but Mair's more for the ballet. And their daddy's a twin, too. Satisfied?'

She seemed to be talking from the far end of an echoing tunnel. Then some giant hand began to shake the bed, to rattle it, to bounce it up and down. Far away in the distance I heard little Hickin say: 'Staff, is she having a rigor?' I remember thinking that at last I knew what it felt like, and that I wished the bed would keep still.

Our G.P., Dr. Payne, called every day when they sent me home. He said I had no idea what 'flu could do to a girl's vitamin B and C reserves, and gave me daily shots of Parentrovite. I'd always thought it was the finest pep-shot in the business until then. For all the good it did me he might as well have injected pink mouthwash. After a week he gave up the unequal battle and told Mother he wanted a second opinion.

'He says your battery's flat,' Freda told me.

'I know.' I had heard him on the landing talking to them.

'He said he'd heard of post-'flu depression, but this was ridiculous. He plans to bring in a trick-cyclist, I gather.'

I suppose she had been deputed to break it to me. She needn't have worried. I said: 'God, I'll see a *vet* if he can get me back on my feet. I'm only half here. It'd be easier to die. The spring's broken.'

'No need for drama, ducky,' Freda said, relieved. 'Living's not so bad, when you're well. Right now, face it, you're sick. Don't lose sight of the fact that everything's temporary. People don't go into declines in this day and age—they bob up again, thanks to modern science and whatnot.'

I began to cry again. It was increasingly easy. 'I don't want modern science, I just want to be me again. I don't feel like me at all.'

'No, of course you don't, pet. But you will, I promise you.' She had been promising me that ever since Father had driven me home, with her to hold my hand.

'Is there anyone you'd actively prefer to see?' Dr. Payne asked next morning. 'Or shall I choose?'

I told him there was just one man I *didn't* want to see—which wasn't strictly true—and that was Dr. Ffestin-

Jones. I also said that I hadn't any objection to his clinical assistant, but that I supposed he wouldn't be allowed to take on domiciliaries.

'You're an S.R.N.,' said Dr. Payne. 'We can always bend the rules a bit in your case. No use being a member of the great and glorious Health Service if you can't have a few privileges. I'll get him here, if that's what you want.'

Rocky came two days later. He had taken the tea-tray from Mother in the hall and brought it up himself. I was glad the cups were thin, the way he liked them. It was one way of beginning the conversation.

He laughed. 'I don't really care whether they're thick or thin, or what colour the brew is. That's just a technique.' He began to pour out. 'When you're coming up towards being a consultant you have to develop a gimmick, or nobody notices you. Like headmasters. You need to be queer about just one thing. One good gimmick and everyone jumps to it over everything else as well. You get a rep as a chap who knows his own mind, notices detail, and raises Cain if he doesn't get his own way. That way fame lies.'

'I see. And what is Dr. Jones's gimmick?'

Rocky looked meditatively into his teacup. 'Jones? I sometimes think his gimmick is not *having* a gimmick. If you see what I mean. Or maybe it's mystery. He does rather like to carry an aura of mystery around with him. Never apologise, never explain, and never let your left hand know what your right hand's up to. Welsh blood, I suppose. Native intrigue.' He lifted his head. 'Mind, I'm not surprised you asked. He was bound to be in your thoughts.' Rocky's eyes were clinical now.

I had no idea what he thought he knew. 'Why should he be? I mentioned him at random. I might as well have said the S.S.O. or Mr. Hutton, or Dr. Watterson.'

'Or the S.M.O.?'

'Oh, no, not him. I know *his* gimmick. Yell at the top of your voice, frighten half the nurses silly, and then yell some more when they make mistakes because they're scared. Oh, and never on any account write legibly.'

'And what does he do when doctors make mistakes?'

'That's different. He doesn't tackle people his own weight. He'd never challenge a man.'

134

'You don't think so? Would you call our Dwyryd a man?'

We were back to square one. 'Naturally. But I don't——'

'He took *him* on.'

'The S.M.O.? How could he?'

'Easily. He's subjected him to a Medical Committee enquiry at any rate. That's fighting talk where I come from.'

I was perturbed. 'When?' The hunch that had been dogging me was right on the surface now, digging its long nails into my back. 'When, Rocky?'

Instead of answering me he leaned back in his chair, and said: 'Ah, so I was right! Tell me, why did you ask to see me?'

'I didn't. It was Dr. Payne's idea.'

'Sorry, I phrased that badly. *When* Dr. Payne wanted you to see what's vulgarly known as a head-shrinker, why did you select me? He said you had.'

'I don't know. So as to make sure he didn't bring Dr. Jones, I suppose.'

'Hm? So? And why didn't you want to see our Dwyryd?'

I blew my nose and played for time. 'Because—well, because he wouldn't much want to see *me*.'

'And why wouldn't he?'

That time I didn't manage any answer at all. I was too busy fishing for a fresh tissue with one hand and trying to balance my cup with the other.

Rocky leaned forward and took the cup and saucer away, and put them back on the tray. 'Because you know he has a damn good reason not to want to see you? A good reason for hating your little guts? Is that it?'

'*No!* And don't shout. Mother'll wonder what's——'

He leaned back again. 'But you do know, Delia. I've just told you.'

'Maybe I'm stupid, but I don't know what you mean.' I was furious with myself for not being able to stop crying. It was humiliating. 'Why don't you tell me?'

'Sweetie, I *have*. About the S.M.O. hauling him up and dropping him in the *schmutz*.'

It was beyond me. 'But how do I come into that?'

'Think. Go on, *think*.'

I tried. 'I *can't* think,' I wailed. 'My head aches.'

'I see. I've got to spell it out to you, have I? ... Well, then, there's a girl named Sinji, a nurse. Yes?'

'Yes.'

'Tell me about her.'

'She's—she's a nice kid. A first-year. She was in Iso with flu, but it knocked her back pretty hard and she developed one of those quick pneumonias.'

'Go on.'

'Well, that's all. Except that the next day the——'

'No, not the next day. That night.'

'That night? Well, Dr. Jones saw her, said it was a true bill, and prescribed for her.'

'That's not strictly true, is it? Tell me *exactly* what happened.'

The hunch had its hands round my throat now. 'Well, Nurse Hickin asked me to look at her. She thought it was pneumonia and she was worried. So I looked at her straight away, and then I gave her a dose of Terramycin. And then Dr. Jones came, and I got him to write it up.'

Rocky sat very still. Only his eyes were awake. 'You say you "got him to". How, precisely?'

I didn't see what he was getting at. 'Well, I didn't exactly have to hit him with the sphyg! I sighed. 'I said I'd given a dose, and if that was O.K. would he write it up.'

'And then? Details now.'

'Then I handed him the case-papers.'

'Folded over to expose the scrip sheet?'

'Naturally.' I hoped my good manners were not in question. I had been trained to treat any senior doctor as a small child, incapable of opening doors, finding the right page in a sheaf of notes, stirring his own tea, or taking down a towel from a rail without assistance. It wasn't likely that I should give any less courtesy to Dr. Jones. 'I always do.'

'And then he wrote it up ... That seems to clear *that* up, then. I didn't understand, before, how anyone as intelligent as he is could possibly have been such a flaming idiot. It was all too simple, after all, wasn't it?'

'A flaming idiot?' I said. 'What would you have given? Dr. Watterson always gives Terramycin.'

'I'm sure he does. And ninety-nine times out of a hundred he'd be right. But not to *that* girl.'

'Oh, really ... *Don't* tell me that coloured girls have

136

different bugs!'

'He wouldn't have given it to the Sinji girl for a very good reason. In her notes it's written in letters half an inch high that *she's allergic to that group of antibiotics*. But you didn't look. And you didn't give poor old Dwyryd the chance to look, either. You folded the sheets back in your obsequious little handmaidenly way—so he'd take it that there were no contra's. Wouldn't he?'

The hunch was rolling about with laughter now. 'Oh *no*!' I said softly. 'No, Rocky!'

'Oh yes. *Now* do you see what you've done?'

'Is that why there was an enquiry?'

'It is.'

'Then why didn't he *say* it was my fault?'

'It puzzles me, too.'

'I ought to have been fetched to the enquiry. Why *didn't* he tell them?'

'You may well ask. I've been asking myself, too, I told you. It doesn't make much sense.'

'Did he tell *you* it was my fault?'

'Not me, nor anyone else. He simply says that he wrote the stuff up off his own bat, that he missed seeing the note about antibiotics, and that he was entirely responsbile for the girl's unfortunate reaction. He was quite unequivocal about it.'

'Then how did you know?'

'It was a process of inspired guesswork. I didn't believe for a moment that he could be so irresponsible, without help. He had only to lift up the case-notes in his hand to see the warning. That argued that he didn't see it because they were handed to him ready folded over by some dedicated little nurse. It *had* to be you. Yet here you are, eating your well-meaning but inefficient heart out, wondering why he can't be bothered with you. Aren't you?'

'You should have told me before.'

'Not my business, sweetie. Not until Dr. Payne hauled me in. How was I to know that he *hadn't* had a slanging match with you? I'd have given you plain hell if you'd done it to me.'

It didn't make sense, any of it. Why had he taken the blame? Not out of any fondness for me: you didn't cut people stone dead if you cared that much about them.

'There was no need,' I said. 'He didn't *have* to take the blame.'

'What would have happened to you if he hadn't?'

'I'd have been suspended, I suppose. Or maybe sacked.'

'For a first offence?'

'But it wasn't——'

'Ah, so you *did* need to be protected. I thought so.'

He took my breath away. Perhaps Rose was right about psychiatrists reading people like books, I thought. Rocky had certainly read me as clearly as he could have read the top type on Mr. Bett's optical chart in O.P. 'You don't miss much, do you?'

'I try not to.'

I told him then all about the sodium amytal row. 'It wasn't serious,' I said. 'Not my part in it, anyhow. But it just shows you how meticulous we have to be, and how strict Matron is.'

'And Dwyryd knew about this business?'

'He knew about Stanway, of course.'

'Then it wouldn't take the brains of Einstein to deduce that everybody involved was due for a rocket.'

I said I supposed not.

'Then given that he made the deduction, mightn't he know too that it'd be worse for you—as a previous offender —than it could be for him? The worst he'd get would be a stiff speech from the chairman of the Medical Committee, and possibly a few drops of poison put down with the Regional people. He couldn't lose his job. After all, the girl didn't die. She was simply made a lot iller and more uncomfortable than she need have been, and that was bad enough. Most S.M.O.s would have had a private word and left it at that. Only a pompous ass like Garthwaite-Roberts would have taken it any further, if it had never happened before. But you could have been thrown out, with a bad reference.'

'You think that's what happened? That he felt he had to shield me, and now he's furious with me for being so incompetent?' I knew that I had only one reason for making the mistake—my eagerness to please Dwyryd. Emotional involvement. What we were all taught to avoid.

Rocky shook his head. 'I wouldn't know. I merely offer it as a suggestion.'

'How can I find out?'

He stood up and jerked down the crumpled corners of his tweed jacket, getting ready to leave me. 'I don't think you need me any more, Delia. Do you? I'll tell Dr. Payne you want to go back to work next week.'

'Rocky! How do I find out?'

He stood in the doorway for a moment. 'Ask him,' he said gently. Then he closed the door.

Freda came up a little later. 'Nice chap,' she said. 'You certainly do collect them at Teddy's.'

'Who? Rocky Walsh? Don't tell me he's asked *you* out.'

'Naturally. We're going skating on Saturday. Why not?'

'No reason at all. He's your sort, actually. And he's "free, white, and twenty-nine", as he puts it. With a hot Mini.'

'I know, I've been looking at it. He says I can drive it.'

'That's what he tells all the girls. And I mean all.'

She looked me over. 'Are you feeling any better for seeing him? That's the point.'

'Better enough to feel like writing some letters. Will you get my pad? It's in the big suitcase, wherever that is.'

'In the boxroom. I'll get it.' When she brought my writing case and pen she said, a little doubtfully: 'You haven't asked about Geoff all week.'

I hadn't even thought about him. 'No. How is he?'

'Still at Queen's. In an ordinary ward now, Isobel says.'

'Isobel?'

'Isobel McKechnie. She rang up to see how *you* were. She'd tried to get you at Teddy's, she said.'

'What for?'

'Well, I suppose she wanted to tell you herself. She—they're engaged, as a matter of fact. I hope you aren't upset? ... No? It's in the *Post* this morning, so I thought maybe you'd want to do something about it ... Like writing with good wishes?'

'I may.' I looked up from the pad. 'I've got a couple of other letters to write first.'

Freda picked up the tea-tray and patted the felt-feathered chicken that was Mother's idea of a tea-cosy. 'Come along, Hickety-Pickety,' she cooed. 'Have you ever had a feeling you weren't wanted, little friend? That makes two of us.'

'Buzz off,' I said rudely.

'There you are—you've had too much vitamin B. You're getting aggressive.' She managed to close the door just before the pillow hit it.

I went downstairs for the first time that evening. My legs felt like pillars of very soggy cottonwool, and my feet hurt after a few steps, but I had to get to the telephone. George was on the switchboard at Teddy's, and he asked how I was before I could get a word in. Then he put me through to Rose. 'She's in Cas, Staff,' he told me. 'And Sister's the other end of the hospital, so it's all right. She hasn't got any casualties in at the moment.'

Rose said: 'Good lord! Voice from the dead!' And then: 'Are you up and about?'

'Not really. I feel pretty woolly. Only I had to come down to ring you. It's your wedding day on Saturday.'

'Correction, *last* Saturday, chum. It's all right—we've postponed it, just for you. You've got a clear fortnight to get yourself fit. After that, Peter says, he's going to "brook no delays". I lost half-a-crown on that, by the way. I said there wasn't a verb to brook. So he looked it up. Seems there's a verb to *not* brook, though, that's never used in the affirmative. Did you know?'

'No,' I said. 'But it'd sound silly if it *was* used in the affirmative. Fancy saying: "Would you brook changing your nights-off, Nurse?" Anyhow, it was your wedding I rang up about. It's a relief to know you're still single.'

'Why?' Rose asked, in what she evidently thought was a low, sinister voice. 'Is he married already? Have you rung to warn me that he's an incurable alcoholic?'

'No, you crackpot! Only I just haven't had the mental energy to write, and I don't really know which day it is yet.'

'I know, poor old thing. Freda told me. She said your battery was pretty flat. Well, that's 'flu, that was. Have they been filling you up with Parentrovite?'

'I can hardly sit down. By the way, Rocky Walsh was here today.'

'Whatever caused that? I must say I haven't noticed him exactly pining for you.'

'I mean, the G.P. got him in.'

'Any help?'

140

'Yes,' I said. 'Quite a lot, actually. Gossipwise, not psychotherapywise.'

'Gossip *can* be psychotherapy. So can cigarettes, love affairs, fast driving, a good boo-hoo or a nice cup of tea. So he told me.'

'He would,' I said. 'Look, he told me why his boss thinks I'm less than the dust.'

'He did? Well, that's something. Why does he?'

'It's too long a story to tell you over the phone. Can you come over?'

'Let's think. I've one night off—tomorrow—if that's any use.'

'Then come,' I told her. 'And stay the night.'

She would, she promised. And she had things to show me. Her ring, for one. Photographs of the flat they'd be living in, in Vancouver. Then I heard an ambulance bell ringing at her end, and the two-tone siren of a police car. 'Here we go,' she said. 'I'm in business. See you.' By the time I had put my receiver down she would be standing calmly at the top of the ramp, looking as though she had been there for a quarter of an hour or more. Any of us who had worked down there had had it rammed into us by Sister Gee that repose was essential, that flustered casualties and their friends would take their cue from us, and that if anyone in her department was caught fussing, flapping, or racing about, she would instantly be banished to the wards. Rose had worked there a good deal, and was extremely good at the rubber-soled, calm efficiency bit. The fact that she might rush into Minor Ops afterwards and cry into a doctors' towel was beside the point: while the emergency was on, and until she had cleared up after it, Miss Nightingale herself could have done no better.

I wished I could go out to the post-box myself, but I knew I should never make it. So I gave Father my letters to post, when he took the dog for his evening walk before supper. He wasn't the kind to so much as glance at the envelopes: if I'd given them to Freda she'd have wanted chapter and verse, and would very likely have succeeded in getting it. I'd done everything I possibly could, and now I had to wait.

It was good to see Rose again. She pushed her ring under

my nose as soon as she came into the room. It wasn't in the Sister Ross bracket, of course, but it was lovely, for all that, an early Victorian cluster of turquoise and pearls on a plaited gold mount. It was exactly right for Rose. 'It's exquisite,' I said. 'Where did you find it?'

'We didn't have to. It belonged to Peter's great-grand-mother. That's why I couldn't have it until it'd been altered for me. Look, here are the photographs. This Professor Finkel, that Peter's replacing, sent them. He's moving out when we move in. He's leaving most of the furniture, because he's going to New Zealand for some reason best known to himself. See—fitted kitchen, central heating ... That's the big living room, with a balcony ... Main bed-room ... Second bedroom ... Bathroom. Like it?'

'It's great,' I said. 'What it is to marry a rich man!'

'Only rich because he'll get two and a half times his Teddy's pay, and twice his Queen's pay, and one and a half times what he'd get as a Queen's consultant. That's to begin with. He gets a pay review after six months. In three years we can put away a nice little nest-egg to come back with.'

'And then?'

'Then we come home, buy a house, and raise a family. What else? That's the object of the exercise, isn't it?'

'All cut and dried,' I said bleakly. 'Rose, I shall miss you. I shall be out on a limb.'

'I'll write. Every week. Now, tell me; what did Rocky tell you? And did he ask Freda out? I'm betting he did.'

'Of course. Skating, on Saturday.'

'He's incorrigible! Still, there's one thing, if he says skat-ing, or driving, or whatever, that's what it'll be. Not looking at etchings. Or so the girls say. He just thinks there's safety in numbers, I suppose.' She perched on the end of my bed and looked expectant. 'Well?'

I told her as tidily as I could, right up to the moment when Rocky left me. 'So now I know,' I finished.

'Is that why he went off on a holiday so unexpectedly? Do you think they suspended him for a week? Could they?'

'They'd be more likely to stop him a month's pay than suspend him. But he could have suspended himself, as it were. Just to withdraw from the scene until it had all simmered down, and while the S.M.O. cooled off.'

'There's not very much you can do about it, is there?'

I wasn't ready to answer that. 'Rose, be a dear and make some tea. I'm parched—and I'm sure you are—and Mother and Freda are both gadding.'

I listened to her rattling crocks' in the kitchen and worked out what I could talk about when she came back. Geoff and Isobel, I thought, would be as good as any other topic to change the subject. If I had made a complete fool of myself, at least I needn't have Rose telling me so.

For two days I watched for the postman from my bedroom window. On the third I got dressed early and watched from the sitting room. On Saturday I overslept, and Mother came up with a cup of tea and two letters. One was blue and square, and the other was a foolscap health service envelope.

'There's a letter from the hospital, I think,' she said. 'I thought I'd better bring it straight up, dear. And I don't know who the other one can be from. One of your hospital friends, perhaps?'

'I expect so.' I took both of them, put them in my lap, and reached for the tea. 'Oh, thank you! The other'll just be my pay-slip, I expect.' I didn't make any move to open them, and after a while she got the message and went away.

I opened the blue one first, to get it out of the way. It was from Isobel McKechnie, thanking me for my good wishes. *They say that after about eighteen months Geoff will probably be able to walk with crutches quite well,* she wrote. *And his father is getting his car converted to hand controls.* She added that they hoped to get married quite soon, so that she could look after him herself, which sounded like sense to me. His mother wasn't capable of looking after a sick cat, in my private opinion. Not that she could be blamed: some women have it, and some don't, and she was one of those who didn't. Isobel wanted me to go to the wedding, at all events, and said that Geoff would write to me nearer the time. Then I read: *If you hadn't been so sweet to me that day at the Queen's I might never have seen Geoff again. I shall always be grateful to you for talking to me as you did, so that I knew exactly where I stood. You ask about the trouble over the flooding—all I know is that Mr. Lockyer has had a lot of workmen there, putting things right at his own expense, and the trouble seems to have died down. My father says that B.R. & L. will probably get the contract for the new comprehensive schools, and that will help to cover the extra outlay. Geoff says it's no use suing Harris for damages, as the man wouldn't be able to pay.*

The wheels within wheels were still functioning, where Mr. Lockyer and Mr. McKechnie were concerned, it seemed. It all left a nasty taste in my mouth, but Isobel sounded too innocent to understand the implications. I hoped she would stay that way, for her own peace of mind. As for Geoff, he seemed to be making progress; and I was glad for him, in a detached and nursish way that had very little to do with the fact that we had once been—or thought ourselves—in love. It all seemed a long time ago, in someone else's life.

I didn't imagine that the second letter would thank me, as Isobel's had, for being truthful. It might even contain a dismissal notice. I handled it and looked at the typewritten address for a good ten minutes before I could bring myself to open it. It was almost certainly the reply I had waited for, yet now I had it I was half afraid to read it. In the end I closed my eyes while I slit the envelope, took out the single sheet, and spread it on my knees.

I need not have worried. The letter itself was hand-written, in the S.M.O.'s awful scrawl, with his florid signature stretching half across the foot of the page:

Dear Miss Jones,

I am grateful for your letter, and I commend you for the courage required to write it. I am afraid that I cannot possibly accede to your request that I should not acquaint Dr. Ffestin-Jones with its contents, for I naturally feel I owe him the courtesy of an apology. I did however simply make it known to him that such and such information had come into my hands, without revealing the source.

I am sure that no reproach of mine can impress upon you more powerfully than can your own self-criticism the importance of the principles involved in the administration of drugs, and of the rules laid down for your guidance in such matters, and I shall therefore offer none. I shall try not to involve you in my plans to see that Dr. Ffestin-Jones is assured of the continuing confidence of the Medical Committee, and I trust that your own health will soon allow you to return to your duties in this hospital. I have not found it necessary to refer the matter to Miss Carte, nor do I propose to do so. I am sure that in future you will exercise a great deal more care.

Yours sincerely,
J. Garthwaite Roberts, M.D., M.R.C.P.

It was typical of him that he had to add his qualifications, and that he wrote so pedantically. He was indeed, as Rocky had said, 'a pompous ass'—but it seemed to me that he had been rather more than fair, and at that moment I had only gratitude for him.

When Mother came up with my breakfast tray a little later she said: 'I don't know what you've got to laugh about—I could hear you right at the other end of the garden! You don't feel *hysterical*, do you?'

'Not really,' I said. 'I just suddenly felt a lot better and I let out a sort of Indian yell, that's all.'

'You're a bit old for that, dear, surely? Still, I'm glad you feel more cheerful. Eat your breakfast, now. This afternoon you might feel like coming to the Conservative garden fête with me. It's a lovely day.'

'Oh, Mother, no! I'd much rather stay in the garden.'

'Well, if you don't *mind* being alone ... Father's got his golf, and Freda's going out somewhere.'

'Skating,' I said, 'with Dr. Walsh.'

'I can't think why people want to go to ice-rinks in the middle of summer. It's not *natural*. Dr. Walsh, did you say? But isn't that the man who came to see you?'

'That's right. He's just right for Freda,' I assured her.

'But, Delia, Freda doesn't know him!'

'Don't worry,' I said. 'She soon will.'

Her bewildered face was as good an excuse as any to laugh again. Poor Mother had never been able to keep track of Freda, ever since she had learned to release herself from her baby reins. She said she really didn't know what girls were coming to these days, and that it was no wonder what so many of them seemed to get into trouble. And that made me think of Miss Baxter, and I laughed all the more.

Father had put the big swing settee under the willow tree at the end of the lawn. It was like being in a yellow–green tent, with the sunlight coming through in narrow ribbons, chalk-striping the turf round my feet. With the canopy pushed away I could lie back and look up at the sky through the whippy green basketwork of branches. I had meant to read, but I closed my eyes against the clear light and went to sleep easily.

The sun was an orange hanging low behind the poplars when I woke. Our old Labrador stood barking on the side path. When he saw that I was awake and moving, he lay flat with his nose on his paws and his big amber eyes watching something just beyond me. I turned to see whether the Post Office tabby was rolling in Father's clump of catmint again, and Dwyryd Jones said: 'Forgive me, Delia. I didn't mean to wake you, *fach*.'

CHAPTER TEN

HE was sitting on the grass, with his arms round his knees, and he was wearing a pale yellow sweater and light blue sailcloth slacks and looked nothing like a doctor at all. Certainly nothing like a respectable consultant. And I can't possibly have been properly awake, or in my normal state of mind, because when he stood up and leaned over me I put up both my arms like a child. He still says that it was I who kissed him first, but it seemed to me that it was something we decided simultaneously. The second time it was certainly he who hunted for my lips, and who said: 'Delia, my *dear* Delia, forgive me.'

I sat up then, and pushed him away so that I could look at him properly, the right way up, and with the golden glow of the sun no longer in my eyes. But I kept my hands on his shoulders, fingering the boyish sweater, so that I could be sure that he was really there. 'Me? Forgive *you*?' I said. 'Oh, darling, what for?'

'For being such a pig-headed prig, for one thing. For not practising what I preach, for another . . . Here am I, telling people—it's my gospel—how important it is to communicate freely, how all their troubles are through lack of communication with themselves and with other folk, and I didn't even speak to you the last time I saw you, much less explain what was happening. Next day, when I wanted to, you were ill. They let me in—in a barrier gown—to look at you, but your eyes hated me . . .'

'No,' I said. 'Dear, that isn't true!'

'To me, it was. I felt guilty, you see. That night, I could at least have put my head into the office and said: "I want to talk to you, *cariad*, but I'm already ten minutes late for a prefect's beating from the S.M.O." Instead, I just walked out. I've been so angry with myself.'

'Angry? Why?' I leaned forward and put my cheek against his. 'This is all wrong.'

'Sweet, whatever you did or didn't do, it was *my* job to check those notes—that girl, Sinji. My job, and mine alone. We pile too many of these responsibilities on to you youngsters, as it is. But you accept them so generously ... we're apt to take them for granted. As I did. As we all do.' He kissed my forehead very gently : it was as though one of the willow leaves had brushed my skin, sunwarm in passing.

I waited for my pulse to settle down, and then I looked at him again. 'Rose said you went away.'

'Yes. I couldn't do my work properly in that state of mind. I need to be calm if I'm to help. So I went home to my lovely river and left Walsh to cope. When I came back you'd been sent home, and I didn't think you'd want to see me. I heard you'd asked for Walsh to see you, and——'

'You're all I've wanted to see for such a long time,' I said. 'Ever since I went to Iso, anyway ... Well, it seems like a long time.'

His kiss then was hard and warm, and it went on for a long time. I didn't see why we ever needed to move again, out of that private moment. Perhaps we wouldn't have done; perhaps we would have stayed there, arrested in sunset light, all night if a car had not stopped at the gate. Even then we turned only our heads, our cheeks pressed together, out of curiosity.

Freda and Rocky came round the corner of the house and froze in mid-step, like children playing Statues. Then Freda came forward, her hand out, laughing, and said : 'Dr. Livingstone-Jones, I presume. Rocky said it was your Volvo in the drive.'

Rocky put his hands on his hips and nodded slowly several times, then lifted his chin in mock disgust. 'So *this* is where you had "an urgent consultation", Chief? It's a small world.' He slid one arm round Freda's shoulders. 'And this is mine. I've decided that she needs a long course of psychotherapy. A *very* long course. The trouble with these Jones girls—as I'm sure you've noticed?—is that they've no insight whatever. Not the slightest clue about the ticking of their own emotions. It's quite absurd. We shall have to educate them intensively, I think.' He grinned. 'Matter of fact, I think all Joneses are a bit afflicted.'

Dwyryd took it very well. He just smiled, and stood up, and ran his fingers through his hair, and said: 'Yes, quite. Well, Walsh, will you kindly get the hell out of my consulting room, and take your patient somewhere else? I'm just about to conduct a rather tricky interview. Thank you.'

When they had gone off, laughing, into the house, he came to sit beside me on the swing and held both my hands between his. 'I've begun at the wrong end, *cariad*,' he said. 'I meant to tell you all about myself first, and then explain how very much I love you. But I've made a mess of it, haven't I? It was your fault—you looked so nice asleep ... There's so much you don't know about me. Where do I begin?'

I put my face into the curve of his neck. 'Hold me,' I said, and then when I was comfortable: 'Do you remember the day you drove me to the flat? When I asked why you didn't fasten your safety belt you said it was a long story. And you winded me, throwing your arm across when you braked, and said it was habit. As though you were used to carrying children with you. And as though you'd had a bad fright, once, and didn't want to talk about it ... So I think maybe there's an accident in this story, a bad one. I don't want you to tell me if it hurts.'

'Go on,' he said quietly. He began to stroke the hair behind my ear. 'What else did you think?'

'That—that maybe it was your fault it happened. Or for some reason you thought it was. And then Rogers said——' I stopped. It didn't matter now.

'Yes?'

'Nothing. It doesn't matter any more.'

'All right, let me tell you. I want to, and you have to know because it's all part of me, of the way I behave, of the person I am. And I love you, Delia, and I want you to know me and accept me as I am ... Are you warm enough, *cariad*?'

'When you say "cariad" do you mean "dear child", or "my darling", or "beloved"?' I asked, remembering Nurse Thomas.

'All three,' he said soberly. 'All three, *fach*.'

'What does "fach" mean?'

'*Fach*? It means "little one".'

'And what is the opposite—big?'

'*Mawr*, masculine. *Fawr*, feminine.' He was amused now.

'Thank you. I shall learn,' I said. 'Go on, *cariad mawr*. How's that?' Then I remembered something else that Rogers had said. 'I do know one thing about you. You're a twin. It's hard to imagine, two people like you. I don't see how there could be.'

His arms tensed quickly, as though he needed something to hold, keeping me close to him. 'That's how the story begins,' he told me. 'Once upon a time there were twins.'

'Identical twins?'

'Identical twin boys. We were very close, the way only twins can be. Like having two selves. My mother was a twin, too, and she and her sister both gave birth in the same week. But we two lived, and Aunt Delyth's baby boy was still-born. So Dewi was brought up by my aunt, and I stayed with my mother. It always seemed right enough to us, until we grew up and other people criticised my mother for "giving away her son".'

'It *was* right,' I agreed. 'Twins are a law unto themselves. What else could she have done?'

'Well, it stopped my aunt from her grief, and it meant one less mouth to feed on my father's pay-packet. He was only a stone-mason, he didn't earn a fortune. Delyth's husband had his own quarry, and he had money to spare for a child. I don't think it was wrong to make four people happier, and give one child a better chance. Anyhow, we lived only half a mile apart, and we still went to school together. And sometimes we'd each go home to the wrong house, just to see how long we could keep it up. My mother could always tell, but Aunt Delyth wasn't so sure.'

'And this was by the river Dwyryd?'

'Yes. Near Tan-y-Bwlch, on the Portmadoc road. Our windows looked at the river and the water-meadows, and we had the hills and woods behind us. My mother still lives there. I shall take you to see her. It's only a stone cottage. I've modernised it for her, because I know she'll never leave it. I can't imagine her happy anywhere else now ... Dewi and I ran along parallel lines all the way—like the *trên bach*, as we call it, the little train that runs along the hill behind the house.'

I did know about that. 'You mean—the Ffestiniog railway, don't you? Did you know that Mr. Marsh, the Hospital Engineer, spends his summer weekends there, working on the extensions? A lot of people go voluntarily, he says. Enthusiasts.'

'God bless them,' he said. 'And did *you* know that it's the only British railway run at a profit?' He was smiling.

'That's a fallacy,' I told him. 'They're not allowing for voluntary labour. But go on, about you and Dewi.'

'We kept together. After school there was university. We both wanted to be doctors. There wasn't a lot of money, but we managed. In the holidays we worked as barmen—Dewi in Portmadoc and I in Criccieth. The visitors couldn't understand how they could see the same barman twice. We had a lot of fun out of that, and sometimes we substituted for one another . . . We qualified on the same day. Then we parted, for the first time.'

'Did you want to? Wasn't it a wrench?'

'It was. But we had to take house jobs where we could get them. We couldn't even get into the same Region. Dewi went to Liverpool, and I came to Birmingham. He wanted to be a physician, but I wasn't at all sure how I'd end. I only knew I didn't want surgery—it didn't go deep enough. It was treating people as bodies without any real life principle. The day Dewi landed a registrarship—while I was still seeking one—he got married. Rhianwen was a lovely girl. She was a staff nurse—like you, *cariad*—and they'd worked together. I got to Liverpool for the wedding, but after that I did a spell on board ship, and I didn't see them for months. When I did . . .' His voice tailed off and his fingers were still in my hair.

I waited for a long moment, and then I said: 'When you did see them?'

'I was just remembering . . .' He began to stroke my hair again. 'When I did, Rhianwen was pregnant. I spent my holidays with them, and when Dewi had night rounds to do I'd stay with her, keep her company. She was nervous, naturally, because she'd been pretty toxic right through, and Dewi thought she might prove eclamptic. He hadn't told her so, but she was too good a nurse not to know the score. One night, when Dewi was at the hospital, she came into labour prematurely. I rang through to tell Dewi, but they said he'd just left. We couldn't wait, so I left a note for him, and put Rhianwen and her suitcase into my car and drove her to the maternity unit.'

'At the same hospital?'

'Oh yes. She wanted to go where she had so many friends. And where she could see Dewi every day. She was very much in love with him, and he was with her, and they hated to be apart.'

'Weren't you ever jealous of her?' I asked him. 'As his twin, I mean? Didn't you feel she got between you?'

'Rhianwen? Lord, no. She was like a twin sister added to us . . . I took her in. Everything happened to delay us. It was a vile night, with driving rain, every traffic light against us too, it seemed. And things weren't normal with her. She couldn't stand the pains at all—I knew there was something wrong. She was screaming aloud before we got there, and that wasn't like Rhianwen. I drove as fast as I dare. There was another hold-up on a sharp bend just before we got to the hospital. Some kind of accident. I could see the police, and the ambulance, and smoke going up behind them, but I didn't dare to stop . . . I ought to have stopped, said I was a doctor, but I had Rhianwen to think of. I felt responsible for her . . . I still blame myself.'

I sat very still and waited for it, for the load of guilt he had been carrying to slip into my lap. When he went on again it came in jerks, not easily, but I didn't interrupt.

'I got Rhianwen in. They took her straight to theatre. A Caesarian—it was locked twins. I waited until all three of them were safe and Rhianwen was sleeping, and then I drove back.' His head moved from side to side, gently, in remembered bewilderment and shock. 'I'd been expecting Dewi to turn up at any minute, you see . . . and he hadn't.'

It was nearly dark now, but Freda had left the curtains open so that the house lights spread just short of the swing. I could see Dwyryd's profile against them. I could hear Rocky's voice and the soft beat of music. I could even hear the infinitesimal sounds of creatures brushing through the grass at our feet. 'Go on, my darling. I'm listening.' I barely breathed it.

'You can guess. When I got to the bend above the hospital where the accident had blocked the road, there was the burned-out wreck of Dewi's car, just being towed away . . . It was his first new one, and he'd been so proud of it. There was a young policeman still there, leaning against the wall, with a white face. I stopped and ran over to him. He'd been sick, he said. Too groggy until then to get back on his motorbike. "It was terrible," he said. "We couldn't release his safety belt in time. The buckle jammed with the heat, and I couldn't get a knife to it in time ... We just had to jump back and watch the flames go up. Thank God the poor devil was unconscious." When I told him it was my brother he began to cry and I cried with him.'

I put both my arms round him. 'I wish I hadn't asked you. I didn't know I was doing this to you.'

'You had to know, Delia ... And I haven't finished.'

'I know,' I said. 'I know, dearest. Do you want to? You don't have to.' But I think I knew that he did, he had to purge himself, once and for all.

'I must. I've never told anyone, except my mother. Not all of it. And even Mother had to be shielded. We didn't let her read the reports of the inquest. It wasn't until then that I knew his neck had been broken as soon as he hit the wall ... That *bloody* safety belt.'

I had never heard him swear, but I felt he was using the only possible word. 'Whiplash fracture?' I said. 'Yes, that's what worries me about them too. I think I'd sooner have a fractured skull than take a chance on that.'

His voice lightened a little. 'Well, now you understand why I never fasten mine ... I want to tell you about Rhianwen. She's the reason for so much in my life, indirectly ... We tried not to tell her that first day. Sister said that Dewi had a streaming cold and that she wasn't allowing him into *her* ward to infect the babies. It didn't wash. She knew. And she didn't want to live at first. Not until they forced her to feed the babies, and made her see that they needed her. She gradually perked up then—but she was never quite the same. She was too quiet. She'd always laughed such a lot, and she didn't any more. Oh, she'd sit smiling, but it didn't go deeper than her lips. She was a good mother, but it was only because she was a good nurse. There was something automatic, impersonal, about the way she'd feed them and wash them, and talk to them.'

'As if they were patients?' I said. I knew what he meant: it was the way I'd felt about Geoff, in that intensive care unit.

153

'Yes. Favourite patients, but patients ... One night she said an odd thing. She said: "Dwy——" People always knew us as Dwy and Dewi, and except to a Welsh ear the distinction isn't easy to hear.' His vowels were clear enough to me: I could hear it. 'She said: "Dwy, if anything ever happened to me you'd look after the children, wouldn't you?" She was pretty casual about it, and I didn't take it very seriously. I said that nothing would happen to her, but that I'd always do anything for the children that Dewi would have wanted. I helped them with money when I could, and I stayed with them when I wasn't on call. I'd got a registrarship myself by then, in Dewi's old firm. The nurses said it was like having him back again, we were so alike in our ways. But my heart wasn't in it, and I'd failed my Primary once.'

I watched Freda come to the French window and peer out towards us, and I willed her to stay indoors.

When she turned back into the room again he went on: 'There was a funny old Night Super up there. I used to have coffee with her sometimes—she liked talking to me. We'd talk about Rhianwen, and Dewi—she'd known them both, you see. She thought the world of Rhianwen, used to go and see her sometimes when she had time. One night she said: "It's a pity you can't marry that girl." It was funny, I'd never thought of Rhianwen like that. To me she was simply part of Dewi, and of me. "She needs someone, she's not well," she said. I said that she'd got me. But it was Dewi she missed. I suppose I was reminding her of him, all the time, and I was too stupid to see it.'

I said: 'Darling, you're shivering. You're cold. Come into the house. Please. You've no jacket on. Don't talk any more now.'

'There's not much more. Stay here, Delia. It won't take long ... Two nights after that the Casualty Officer came up to the ward, looking for me. I don't think he'd been up there in years. He looked lost. He took me into the clinical room and sat me down, and told me that he'd just had Rhianwen brought up to Cas. The ambulance men hadn't been able to resuscitate her, and she'd been dead on arrival ... She'd gone out in her old car—it was one I'd bought from my houseman for her—and run it straight into the wall, two yards from the place where Dewi's had landed, on the bend. They called it "accidental death" at the inquest, but I knew it wasn't ... When the C.O. had gone I went down to see old Sister Fazakerley. She was the only one I could tell. Do you know what she did?'

'Made tea and comforted you, I hope. What else?' I said. 'What else *could* she do?'

'Is that what you think? She raged at me. She said it was all my fault. That any fool but me could have seen that Rhianwen was in an acute depression. that she was a suicide risk. She'd been a psychiatric nurse, and she knew what she was talking about. She said she'd tried to warn me, over and over again, but that I never listened.'

'How *unfair*!' I said. 'Just how cruel can old women be?'

'*Cariad*, she was right. And I'm glad she did it. She changed my life. Don't you see, I'd been so ignorant, and Rhianwen was dead because of it. It *was* my fault—I should have seen, and got her the help she needed. They teach us so little about these things when we train! I'd never *heard* of "smiling depression", much less seen it. Nowadays, every G.P. is beginning to realise, and to learn, because fifty per cent of his patients, at least, are needing psychological help. But as little as five years ago, I was so ignorant that I let Rhianwen die. She could have been cured.'

I had to take the weight away from him somehow. 'Dear, I don't think she'd have wanted to be. She wanted to be with Dewi, and without him life wasn't worth having. I'd feel the same myself. If I—— If I lost someone like that *I* wouldn't want any second-best tranquillised life. You weren't meant to help her, I dare say.'

'It's easy to say that now.'

'It's easy to blame yourself, too.'

He looked at me then, searching my eyes. 'I hadn't seen it like that. As a line of least resistance. Dramatising things, so that I could wallow in them.'

'I didn't put it that way. But it *is* easy to feel guilty about things. I do it myself. It's that old Fazakerley's fault!'

'No, she was right. Because I saw then what it was I wanted to do. What I *had* to do. I transferred to a psychiatry as quickly as I could. My mother had the children while I took my D.P.M.—both Rhianwen's parents were dead. Now

I have them with me at Four Oaks: they're too much for my mother to have them all the time, and I wanted them close to me. They go to school there, and I have a nice motherly housekeeper who gives them a great deal of affection. It was the best I could do for them.' He smiled. 'My mother insists on having them during the holidays. They're there now. I saw them a month ago when I went up. Next week I have to bring them back.'

The lights of Father's car swung across the lawn and died. I could hear Mother's voice too. She would be asking whose were the cars outside, and putting on her special face to greet her daughters' followers, smiling a little anxiously.

He stood up then, and pulled me to my feet. 'They're lovely little girls, Delia . . . You're cold, my dear.'

I leaned close to him. 'Do you want to go away quietly? Or would you like to meet my parents? They're very nice, really. Mother fusses a bit, but mothers do.'

He looked down at me with his hands on my shoulders. 'I know. So does mine. She thinks I don't eat enough, or wear enough clothes. She'll never believe I'm capable of choosing a wife for myself.'

'And are you?'

'I shall tell her that you chose me . . . Delia, you are going to marry me, aren't you? Will you mind having the twins thrown in? I tried to adopt them, but I'm not allowed to until I have a wife. We can make them legally ours when we're married.'

I wanted to laugh, cry, sing and dance, all at once. Instead I said: 'Oh, so *that's* all you want me for, is it? Just so that you can adopt the twins? Charming!' Then I added: 'Darling, they'll be an unexpected bonus. But will they like *me?*'

He said that they had better, or he'd stop their pocket-money for at least a fortnight. He seemed as light-hearted as I was feeling. Then we went into the house, blinking in the light.

Rocky and Freda must have prepared the ground for us, because Mother was out in the kitchen, a little weepy, and kissed me unexpectedly when I went to fetch another cup. We didn't have to tell them anything: they all took it for granted. But Dwyryd insisted on asking Father, very formally, whether he had any objections. Father—whose humour is a little heavy-handed, so that some people don't see it—said that girls seemed to do as they liked these days, but that at least I'd had the sense to pick another Jones, and he hoped he could keep up with us. Mother cried openly, and kissed Dwyryd twice by mistake. Freda yelled: 'Yippee! Now we'll all be able to get psychoanalysed free of charge!' Rocky told her she had her own psychiatrist and that it was highly unethical to go to another. Then Father fetched out the last two bottles of champagne—we'd had them in the cellar ever since I'd had an engagement party with Geoff. That seemed long ago, in someone else's history, not mine at all. We all got a little tipsy, and Rocky and Freda insisted on going on to the lawn to pour a libation to the gods. Suddenly it had become a lovely evening.

I went out to the gate with Dwyryd, after Rocky had roared away, and Freda had gone up to her room. It must have been long after midnight. He said: 'Then it's settled? Next week you'll come with me to fetch Catrin and Mair, and tell my mother. The week after, you go back to work and give in your month's notice?'

'Not yet,' I insisted. 'I want to work until I'm married, even if it is to be quite soon. I'd *really* like to work after that, too, just for a little while. Couldn't I? You'll need an S.R.N. for all this biochem research you're planning, however many R.M.N.s you import. And Sister Ross is going soon. You see, I could train somebody to do it for you, before I left.'

When I'd talked to Geoff about working after marriage he had been horrified. People would think that he couldn't afford to keep me, he'd said. Dwyryd didn't react that way at all. He said: 'You shall do whatever you want, *cariad*. For a year, if you like. After that . . .' His kiss told me that we both had the same kind of plans for the future. Then he said: 'There's one thing we haven't talked about.'

'What's that?'

'Where shall we live?'

'You mean there's a choice? I thought we'd be——'

'Of course there's a choice. I'm a man of many mansions now! Three, with the cottage. I've bought the Guerdon Road house.'

I hadn't thought it possible that he could bring up yet one

more surprise, but that was totally unexpected. 'You've
what?'

'Well, the man who owned it said that he was selling it,
and that it wasn't legal for me to be there anyway, and that
I'd have to get out of the flat. The other chaps would have
to go too. A fellow named McKechnie. But I'm Welsh, and
we Welsh enjoy a little haggle. So I said: "All right, I'll
offer you a hundred more than he does." And he agreed.
don't think he'd expected that at all.'

I began to laugh, and he wanted to know what was so
funny. I said: 'It's a long story, darling. Not as long as
yours, but too long for now. Remind me to tell you next
week, on the way up to Wales.'

'I will,' he promised. 'Then we can talk about the house,
as well.' He kissed me once more. 'Good night, cariad.'

I said: 'Nos da, my darling.'

I wanted to tell him to drive carefully, but I didn't. I
knew that as long as we lived that was the one thing I need
never do. So I stood there watching the tail-lights of the
Volvo tinsel their way along A38 until they disappeared.
Then everything was very still, and there was nothing to
see but a few stars. I was the last to go to bed that night,
and the last to sleep, but I knew I should wake early to
being living all over again. This time it was right. This time
I had no doubts at all. What was more, I was well again.

It was only then, I think, that I knew how much I had
had in common with Rhianwen, that I had not been physi-
cally ill at all but made sick by my depression. It seemed a
pity that Dr. Payne had wasted so much Parentrovite on
me, if all the cure I needed was a quiet talk with Dwyryd.
Rose was right, as usual. Love is good psychotherapy. The
best, probably.

To our devoted Harlequin Readers:

Here are twenty-four titles which have never been available from Simon & Schuster previously.

Fill in handy coupon below and send off this page.

Harlequin Romances

TITLES STILL IN PRINT

~~~~~~~~~~~~~~~~~~~~~~~~~~~~

Harlequin Books, Dept. Z

Simon & Schuster, Inc., 11 West 39th St.
New York, N.Y. 10018

☐ Please send me information about Harlequin Romance Subscribers Club.

Send me titles checked above. I enclose .50 per copy plus .15 per book for postage and handling.

Name ....

Address ....

City .... State .... Zip ....

MAIL THIS COUPON TODAY